Feisty Scholar Publications

www.feistyscholar.com

Copyright © Cher L. Jones 2023

No part of this publication may be stored within a retrieval system or device, transmitted or reproduced by any means, without the prior written permission of the author.

All rights are reserved.

Jump

First Edition

978-1-913619-20-6 (*eBook*)

978-1-913619-25-1 (*Paperback*)

Cover designed by Mibl Art

For news and details of upcoming publications from this author visit:

www.cherjones.co.uk

Chapter One

A halo of light hovers above me. It's too bright, and I flinch away. When I risk a peek at the room, every surface gleams a sterile white. The scrubs I wear are as devoid of colour as the rest of the room, as if I'm trying to camouflage myself.

I search for a memory to anchor me. A relative, my favourite song, even what I had for breakfast this morning would be something. But my mind won't cooperate.

Panic swells in my chest and adrenaline forces me into motion. I try to sit up, but the resistance from the wires attached to my forehead and the straps encircling my wrists pulls me back into the chair. I tug at the restraints, and they bite into my arms.

'Stop struggling.'

I crane my neck to look for the source of the voice, but she is just outside my peripheral vision. 'Where am I?'

The same woman speaks into my right ear, close enough

that the warmth of her breath gives me shivers. 'In the facility. That's all you need to know.'

I twist and buck. 'Let me go!'

'Ryan, calm down. You're going to hurt yourself.'

'Ryan?' The name feels strange on my lips, but my mind doesn't offer another to slot into its place.

'Relax.' She rips open the Velcro straps. 'We'll soon have you out of here.'

Although the restraints weren't particularly tight, my struggle has caused red rings to form around each wrist, and I massage them. 'Who are you?'

'Andrea.' A smirk tugs up the side of her mouth. 'But that isn't what you really want to ask, is it?'

'Who...who am I and what am I doing here?'

She kneels next to me. Her hair is an unnatural red and pulled into a messy ponytail. It's a stark contrast to the dull grey scrubs she wears. 'You are—' Her sentence is cut off when the door opens, and she darts to a machine on the other side of the room.

A man enters but she doesn't register his presence. Instead, she continues to punch buttons.

'Give us a minute, please, Andrea,' he says.

Her eyes flicker in my direction. 'That's not the procedure.'

'Time is running out. Please, I won't be long.'

Her hesitation gives way to a nod, and she leaves the room.

The man drags a wooden chair from the side of the room, and he sits. His suit looks stiff and uncomfortable, as though it's the starch in it that holds his back so straight.

He stares at me, unblinking. 'Well?'

Although I am relieved the silence has been broken, I have no idea how to respond. 'Well, what?'

He snorts out a puff of air. 'I don't have time for this. What did you learn from the jump?'

'The jump?' I must sound ridiculous, parroting his every word, but I don't know what else to say.

'Yes, what did you see?'

I scour my brain, and images begin to surface.

A tiny bird of a woman stands in front of me, wracked with sobs, muffling her gasps with a balled handkerchief. Her eyes flick up and meet mine. They are a startling blue next to the pinked whites and puffy moons of flesh beneath her eye sockets; she must have been crying for some time. Despite this, she is beautiful. Her thick blonde hair is twisted into a knot. The corners of her mouth are tugged down, but still, I can't help noticing the perfect bow of her lips.

'A woman,' I offer. 'She was blonde.'

'Ground breaking,' he says, his tone devoid of enthusiasm. 'And?'

A building of sweeping marble and pillars with curled tops stands in front of us. It's a mausoleum. The graves spattering the ground around it give it away.

'I think I was at a funeral.'

'Keep going.'

'I don't know what you want from me.'

His top lip jerks up in a snarl. 'I want something that proves you aren't wasting all our time here.'

'I'm trying to remember. Really, I am.' I close my eyes and try to focus, which is difficult when his disdain simmers so relentlessly next to me.

The woman holds out her arms to me and dissolves into sobs. Her tears seep through my blouse. 'Mom,' she says.

Mom? That can't be right. Behind her back, I examine my hand. The nails are manicured in a blood red, and a diamond, fat and sparkling, sits on my wedding finger. But money can't buy youth, I think, looking at the liver spots jostling for space on my skin. I'm sure if I pinched it, I'd leave stubborn peaks.

I hold out my own hand, and I'm relieved to find the skin pale and flawless. 'This is going to sound crazy, but in my dream, memory, whatever it was, I was that woman's mother.'

'Yes, Edith Hudson; we know all of that. Was there anything suspicious about the people around you?'

Over her shoulder, I see we are surrounded by mourners. From their tear-stained cheeks to the strings of snot dripping from reddened noses, their grief is suffocating.

'No. They were just...mourning.'

Flags of colour rise in his cheeks. 'You are wasting—'

'Detective Reynolds, he's told you what he knows.' Andrea is back, although she slotted into the exchange so swiftly that I suspect she was loitering just outside the door.

Reynolds looks her up and down. 'Why would he remember so little? There must be more that he isn't telling us.'

'It happens sometimes. Just give him some time to orientate himself.'

Reynolds buttons his jacket as he gets to his feet. 'Fine. But make it quick. We need answers.'

'I don't think he likes me,' I say once he's out of sight.

Andrea's laugh is flat. 'I wouldn't worry about that. He doesn't like anybody.'

'Do you like me?'

Our eyes lock, and she gives this some thought, before heading back to her machine. 'I don't know you.'

'I'm new, then?'

That same mirthless snigger. 'Brand new.'

'What is it I do here?'

Andrea spins around so fast that her ponytail swings from side to side. 'You look for clues from the past.' She sweeps a hand above a control panel covered in blinking lights. 'All of this technology lets you go back and experience events through the eyes of the witnesses.'

'I remember being an old woman. My hand...it was wrinkled.'

'Don't you worry. Your skin is soft as a baby's bottom. But I wouldn't say Edith was old. She would have been in her fifties then.'

'And I was her?'

'That's right.'

This information should feel jarring to me, but my subconscious tells me it's true. I suspect it's something that has been explained to me many times. I can tell by the way she reels off this information without pausing that Andrea has said it more than once.

'So, I'm a detective, then?'

'Sure, of sorts, I suppose.' She is busying herself with the machine again.

'And I work with Reynolds.'

'Alongside would be a better description. He is investigating the same crime in the more traditional way. He has been for years. Maybe that's why he's so grumpy all the time; he's worried you will discover something he couldn't.'

'Or maybe he's just an ass.'

'Also a likely possibility. But anyway, that pretty much sums up what you do here. You look for clues, and he follows up on them. At least he would, if you'd found any.'

'Wouldn't it be easier if he just looked for the clues himself?'

'He can't do what you do.'

'Jump?'

'That's right. You have a slightly bigger hippocampus than most. That's the part of the brain where memories are stored. With a little chemical manipulation from us, you're able to assimilate memories from other people, times and places.'

'I've often been admired for my large hippocampus.'

Andrea rolls her eyes.

'Sorry. I guess I make bad jokes when I'm nervous.'

'It's not that; though it was a bad joke. You said the same thing last time you jumped.'

'Oh.' Embarrassed, I change the subject. 'So, what now?'

'Next, you talk to the Professor.'

Chapter Two

I fidget under his gaze. 'Why do they call you the Professor?'

His hands are steepled. 'Because I'm a professor.'

'Right. Makes sense.' I feel more stupid with each word I utter. 'Have we met before?'

He leans forward as if I'd said something that interested him. 'Why do you ask?'

'I couldn't answer that detective's questions. Andrea said I have some memory loss. So, I thought maybe we'd met, and I just don't remember.'

'Reynolds shouldn't have even been talking to you. I ask the questions. Andrea needs to do her job.'

Guilt gnaws at my stomach. She has been kind to me, and by the sounds of it, I've got her in trouble. 'It wasn't her fault. Reynolds didn't give her much choice.'

The Professor sniffs but drops the subject. 'In answer to your question, yes, we've met before. Today was your second jump. I questioned you after the first.'

'I don't remember that.'

He looks at me long enough for me to feel uncomfortable again. 'Well, don't be concerned. We are manipulating the areas of your brain that deal with memory. Temporary amnesia is a predictable side effect of that. We hope the training we give counteracts it, but some jumpers are more successful than others.'

Already I'm disappointing him. 'Okay. So how does all of this work?'

'The jumps? Atomic transition. Or in layman's terms, quantum leaps.'

I muse at his use of 'layman' and feel more stupid than ever.

'The transition of energy from one state to another.' He adds this as though it should clarify it for me.

I remain silent.

'The quantum leap allows the energy in your brain to move from the present to the past. Your energy temporarily takes the place of that of the person you are jumping into.'

'Oh! Like the television show!'

His eyes narrow. 'You remember that?'

A memory rises from the darkness.

I sit wedged between two people (my parents?), a bowl of popcorn on my lap, while we watch reruns. My feet dangle over the edge of the sofa, and I kick them with excitement as the theme music begins.

'I guess my memory is coming back.' I'm pleased to have some remnant of my past, even if it is from a cult eighties show that finished decades before I was even born.

'It appears so. Don't push it though. Each jump causes a mini trauma to your brain. We don't want to exacerbate that.'

I consider this. 'You said temporary amnesia. Could this be dangerous for me?'

He shrugs off my question. 'The risks are minimal, and you are compensated handsomely for them. You volunteered for the role. I have copies of all the signed paperwork. Would you like to see them?'

He heads for the filing cabinet at the side of the room and takes out a brown folder.

Somewhere, a part of my mind is demanding that I shut up. 'No, it's fine.'

'If you're having second thoughts, there are hundreds of candidates more than willing...'

'No, I'm not. It's just a little disorientating, not being able to remember anything.'

The Professor hesitates, I suspect for effect, before he slides the cabinet drawer closed. 'If you're sure. Because we do have backup jumpers ready to...'

'Really, it's fine. I get it; I need you more than you need me. I don't doubt that.'

He doesn't answer but his fleeting smirk is all the confirmation I need. 'Well, at least let me answer some of your questions.' He flips open the file. 'Would a mini-biography help? Ryan Smith. Twenty years old. Parents – Lydia and James Smith. You're an only child. You live in a rented studio apartment on the other side of the city.' He does not attempt to hide his boredom as he reels off these facts. 'What else would you like to know?'

'I suppose I'm still wondering *why*? On that last jump, I was in the body of an old woman.'

'Old is a subjective term. But yes, Edith Hudson. The victim's mother-in-law.'

'Okay. But what was the point in jumping into her?'

He takes off his glasses. 'Well, that bit is down to you. We just handle the science. It's your job to look for clues.'

'Clues about what?'

'A murder. Or at least that was the official ruling in the end. Robert Lyle's body was never recovered. However, there were signs of a struggle in his office that would indicate he was taken by force.'

'But I was at his funeral.'

The Professor shakes his head. 'It was just a memorial service. They added his name to the marker on the Hudson mausoleum and held a ceremony, but there was no body.'

'Hudson?'

'It is his wife Julia's family that has the money. It's their crypt. Although, once he married into the family, he held his own. He worked very closely with her father.'

'Was Julia blonde? I think I might have seen her on the last jump.'

'Yes, that would have been her. She was with Edith at the service. What else can you remember?'

'I'm sorry. Like I told the detective, I didn't see anything unusual. Just a lot of crying people.'

The Professor purses his lips. 'Okay. Then what did you feel when you jumped into her?'

'I don't know. Confused, I guess.'

'Not you; your host, Edith. Did you notice any physiological symptoms that suggested any type of emotion? Was she crying; was her heart beating fast? That kind of thing.'

I wrack my brain. 'Nothing really. I guess I was a bit overwhelmed with my own feelings.'

He sits back in his chair. 'A wasted jump, then.'

I scour my brain for something useful to share. 'Perhaps they didn't get on. I don't think she felt particularly sad. Surely I would have picked up on that?'

He sighs. 'The Hudsons loved Robert.'

'Send me back. Maybe I missed something.'

'No. We can only let you jump a finite number of times before you are at risk of permanent damage. We can't waste them on dead ends.'

'Okay. I'll do better on the next one.'

He gives me a broad smile that doesn't reach his eyes. 'Let's hope so.'

Chapter Three

Andrea is waiting for me outside the door. 'How did it go?'

'I'm pretty sure he thinks I'm an idiot and wants to fire me.'

'Well, you've got five more jumps to impress him.'

'Five? That's it?'

'Yep. One jump a day for a week. Easiest money you ever made.'

'Oh.' This isn't a career, then; just a way to make some quick cash. I'm surprised to find I'm a bit disappointed, considering that a couple of hours ago I knew nothing of jumping or this place. I still don't really.

'Cheer up. You'll be able to pay off those student loans, put a deposit on an apartment, maybe even have a holiday.'

'I told you about my loans?' Not that I remember them myself. But debt seems a pretty heavy subject to discuss with someone I've known for two days.

'Sorry. I didn't mean to make you feel uncomfortable.'

She has, but as the only friendly face I've encountered, I decide not to dwell on it. 'It's fine. Is there somewhere I can get some food? It feels like my stomach is about to eat itself.'

'Of course. I should have thought.' She stumbles over her apology.

'I just learned I'm twenty years old, which I'm assuming rules you out as being my mother?'

'I'm twenty-five, you ass.' She thumps me on the shoulder. 'Come on, I'll show you where the canteen is.'

The canteen is lit with a harsh light that hurts my eyes. We cross a checkerboard of floor tiles and join the queue. I put two packaged sandwiches on my tray.

'You are hungry,' Andrea says.

When I reach the register, I search my pockets for my wallet. 'I must have lost it.' My face burns.

'Yeah, that's what they all say.' Andrea hands the cashier her staff lanyard and she swipes it to pay for my food.

'No. Thank you, but I can't let you do that.'

'Ryan, it's fine; I'm messing with you. The canteen doesn't take cash and your meals are included with the job. I'm supposed to make sure you're fed.'

The shame gripping my chest loosens.

I scan the canteen and realise that everybody is sitting in twos. 'Are these people jumpers, too?'

'Jumpers and technicians. Jumpers wear white, technicians wear grey.' She flaps a hand back towards the cashier. 'Domestic staff wear navy blue.'

'The jumpers and technicians eat together?'

Andrea nods towards a vacant table, and I follow her to it. 'It's part of our job description. We make sure the jumpers are comfortable during their stay, get them anything they need, ensure they make their appointments...'

'So less like a mother and more like a babysitter then?'

She gives me a half grin. 'Without me, you'd still be sitting in that chair trying to remember your name.'

I can't argue with that. 'So, do we live together for this week?'

'Sorry, Casanova. I clock out at five.'

'I didn't mean it like that.' I feel the heat rising in my cheeks again.

'Stop taking everything so seriously. No, you stay in one of the facility units. Your only job in the evenings is to rest in preparation for the next day's jump.'

'That sounds pretty dull.'

'Probably, but it's only for a week. You'll survive.'

Close to our table, a man dressed in blue sloshes a mop across the floor. It is only when he nods a hello that I realise I've been staring.

I give him an awkward wave in return. Andrea looks over her shoulder to see who I am looking at, but he has already moved from her line of sight.

Besides, we both have our attention drawn towards raised voices on the other side of the canteen. A short, tanned man, almost as wide as he is tall, stands and flips his tray. The cooked meal creates a Jackson Pollock effect on the tabletop.

'You can't keep me here.' He smashes his fists down, smearing the food.

The man with him, who I assume is his technician, stands with his palms raised. 'Lloyd, we talked about this.

Nobody is holding you against your will. You signed up for this.'

A low growl bursts from Lloyd's throat as he runs at him. Although he is at least a foot shorter than the technician, his bulk is pure muscle.

The taller man is pinned against the wall, staring wide-eyed down into the face of his charge. Stumpy fingers encircle his throat.

Andrea gets to her feet and gathers the food from my tray. 'Let's make these sandwiches to go.'

'We should help him.' I take a tentative step towards the choking man.

'He already has help. Security is on it.'

Two men, dressed in shirts and trousers in the same grey as Andrea's scrubs, try to hoist the man off.

Lloyd squeezes harder. The technician's eyes bulge and his face glistens with a sweaty sheen.

'Come on.' Andrea is tugging at my arm.

As we reach the exit, I hear an ominous buzz and Lloyd jerks backwards. He crumples to the floor, twitching.

'They tasered him.'

Andrea's eyebrows shoot up. 'Wouldn't you?'

I take her question as rhetorical. 'What was wrong with him?'

'People handle the drugs and the trauma caused by the jumps in different ways. You suffered memory loss. He...'

'Turned homicidal.'

'Yeah.' She swallows hard and I wonder what it is like for her, wondering after each jump what the person waking up in that chair will be like. Wondering if she is safe.

'He can't have been stable to start with.' What I really

want to say is, *You don't need to be afraid; I'm not like him.* But I don't, because in truth I have no evidence to support that claim.

We push through a double set of doors. An orderly is coming the other way and I wedge the door open with my foot so he can pass.

'Thank you,' he says. It is only as he passes that I notice the stubble and salt and pepper of his greying hair; it is the same man who was mopping in the canteen.

Andrea stops on the other side of the door, waiting for me to join her. 'Are you okay?'

'Yeah, I'm fine.' I'm puzzling over how the orderly managed to get ahead of us, but I can see by the easy way Andrea navigates the facility that she, too, likely knows all the shortcuts. 'Where are you taking me?'

We are striding down a white corridor filled with an overpowering smell of bleach. Doors line its sides.

'To your unit.'

'I thought you said I would go to my unit at five. Is it time already?'

'No but after that display in the canteen, they're bound to call a—' An alarm bisects her sentence. 'A lockdown.' She grimaces against the shrill bleat that bounces around the corridor.

Finally, she stops in front of one of the doors. 'R Smith' is written in wipeable marker on a nameplate on the door. It confirms that my stay is transient; in less than a week I'll be wiped away.

'This is your unit.' She opens the door with her keycard and flaps me inside. 'I'll be back in the morning to escort you to the lab for your next jump. Be ready.' Her voice is raised to combat the noise and she presses her fingers against one ear. 'Try to get some rest.'

Then she pulls the door closed. Even over the alarm, I hear the clunk. I try the handle but the door doesn't budge. I'm locked in.

Chapter Four

The frosted glass of what pretends to be a window casts an eternal twilight on the room, making it impossible to estimate the time. At no point during the night did it dim, so I doubt it's the outside world on the other side.

There is no clock in my unit, so, to make sure I'm not late, I get dressed as soon as I wake.

I search the room for something to do. The shelves are lined with books, but when I investigate them, I find rows of bland classics that don't appeal to me. As there is no other option, I randomly select one and sit on the bed. After just a few pages of *Pride and Prejudice*, I discard the novel on the bedside table and sit watching the door.

When the handle finally rattles, I spring to my feet.

'Morning.' Andrea carries in a tray and places it on the bed in front of me. 'How did you sleep?'

'Fine,' I lie. 'What's this?' I scoop up a spoonful of the stodgy contents and then let it drop back into the bowl.

Andrea claps me on the shoulder. 'Everything a growing lad needs.'

My spoon clatters onto the tray. 'No thanks.'

'Suit yourself. Are you ready to go?'

'Definitely. I'm determined to do better today.'

Andrea is already leading me from the room. 'You will. Try not to put too much pressure on yourself.'

'Where...who will I be jumping into?'

'Martin Hudson; the victim's father-in-law.'

'They think he might have done it?'

Andrea presses her lips together to suppress a chuckle, but it escapes in little puffs of air from her nose. 'Unlikely. I don't think he'd be bankrolling all of this if he was guilty.'

It hadn't occurred to me that there would be a driving force behind my jumps, other than justice.

As if reading my mind, she says, 'Had anybody else disappeared like that, the police would have chalked it up to a tragedy, left the case open, and told the family to get on with their lives. Not if you're a Hudson, though. If you have enough money to throw at a case, it will never go cold.'

We reach the lab and she nods towards the chair. 'Take a seat.' She fastens the Velcro over my wrists.

'Is that really necessary?'

Her eyebrows knit. 'You did see that guy in the canteen, right?'

'Yeah, but I don't have that in me.' I hold my head up, defiant, waiting for her to argue that there is no way for me to know.

She is silent as she readies the injection. Then she says, 'Ryan, don't get me wrong. You seem nice enough. But I'd put money on it that Lloyd said much the same thing.'

'Whatever. So what do I do once I get there?'

'You don't *do* anything. You just feel and observe.'

'But when I saw the Professor, he said...' I think back to our conversation, doubting my recollection. 'I thought it was like *Quantum Leap*.'

She gives a slow blink.

'You know, the TV show?'

'Oh, I know it. And the Professor told you it was like *Quantum Leap*?' The po face she has assumed begins to crumble and is replaced with a grin.

'Well, no. I just...Shut up,' I say, although I'm smiling too.

'There's nothing for you to do. Everything you will see has already happened. If we could really change anything, we'd be locking Robert Lyle in a cupboard for his own safety, not investigating his murder. Feel and observe; they're your only two jobs.'

'Okay.' I settle back into the chair. 'I can do that.'

A sharp scratch forces a shriek from me. I look down to see a needle puncturing my bicep. 'You could have warned me.'

'Sorry. I thought it might be easier on you if you didn't see the injection coming.'

I rub my arm. 'Did that tactic work yesterday?'

If she answers, I don't hear it. Already my vision is swimming.

Andrea attaches something to my temples.

'What are you doing?' I ask, although my words bleed into one another.

'Just close your eyes.'

Her instruction confuses me; how am I supposed to observe anything if my eyes are closed? I follow it anyway.

I see only black. Then colours and shapes begin to flash before me like I've forced my lids together too hard. The shapes float together, as though magnetised, and a picture starts to form.

I think back to an art class I took as a child. We were taught to draw people using basic shapes. That is how the world in front of me is being built. An oval slots onto a square, which in turn sits on top of a...trapezium? Rhombus? I can never keep them straight. Then detail is added, as though some mad artist is frantically scribbling. The oval becomes a face. The outstretched oblong is a hand, and I'm shaking it.

'Rob! Good to see you. Take a seat.' The words come out of my mouth, but it isn't my voice. These vocal cords are strained and rasping, the victim of too many cigarettes.

I walk towards a sleek leather settee. My legs move without my authority and make me think of that animation where the unsuspecting man and his dog are taken hostage by a pair of mechanical trousers. This makes me want to laugh, which then makes me wonder if that laugh would come out of Hudson's mouth.

I order myself to focus. Martin Hudson, I'm Martin Hudson.

I sit on the settee. The office around me is decorated in rich, dark wood. I start thinking about the fact that I'd never be able to afford anything like this but then berate myself. Concentrate.

'So, what was it you wanted to talk to me about?'

Martin turns our head towards Robert. 'Straight to business, huh? First things first, I wanted to ask you about Luke.'

'Luke? What about him?'

Hudson shifts so that the polished leather squeaks. He takes a deep breath. 'I know he's been your friend for more years than I've known you, but are you sure he can be trusted?'

Robert gives the slightest flinch. 'Of course. I've known him for twenty years. I trust him with my life.'

Martin is nodding and I can hear the gristly protest of his neck. 'I'm not going to sugar coat it; we've found some irregularities with his accounts.'

Robert's eyes widen. 'It's not possible. A mistake, I'm sure. I'll look into it personally.'

'I know you will. What else do I keep you around for?'

The office door opens, and a woman enters. There is no doubt she is stunning. Almond eyes peer out behind a sheet of silky black hair.

I'm disturbed to realise that Martin finds her attractive, too. His eyes track her figure up and down and his pulse quickens.

'I'm sorry,' she says. 'I'll come back.'

'Not at all,' Martin says. 'Robert, you've met Leona?'

'Many times.' Robert nods a hello, but his back is to me so I can't judge his response.

Leona walks backwards towards the door, her palms raised. 'Really, it's fine. You finish up. I've got some paperwork to drop off at accounting anyway. I'll come back in ten.'

Robert stares after her for longer than is necessary.

'Gorgeous, isn't she?' Martin asks.

This jerks Robert from whatever daydream he was in. 'I hadn't really noticed.'

Martin clenches his teeth so hard that I feel his jaw tic. 'Don't insult my intelligence. I've heard the rumours.'

Robert's mouth opens and closes like a goldfish, but he says nothing.

Martin heads for the decanter of scotch on the other side of the room and pours himself a glass. When he takes a sip, my mind does combat with itself, part of it savouring the oaky warmth, the other wanting to spit the burning liquid over the cream carpet.

'You think I double-booked you two by accident? I wanted to see your reaction.'

'I...I don't know what to say.' Robert has turned two shades paler in the time it took Martin to pour the drink.

'You don't need to say anything. I wouldn't believe you even if you did. But it ends now. Do you understand me? This second. Leona is being transferred to the New York office, although she doesn't know that yet. And you are going to have a long and happy marriage with Julia.'

Robert is staring at his shoes as though they might provide him with some kind of answer. 'You have my word. I'm sorry I've let you down, Martin.'

'Hurt my daughter, and you'll find out the true meaning of the word 'sorry'.'

Martin knocks back the rest of his drink. As the burning in my throat begins to subside, the world around me starts to fade.

Chapter Five

'It was Martin Hudson. He killed Robert Lyle.'

The Professor cocks his head to one side. 'Really? And what evidence do you have for this?'

'Just think about it; what better way to throw us off the scent than by pretending he's desperate to find his son-in-law's killer?'

'An interesting theory, but you're wrong.'

'I'm not. You weren't there. He was furious with Robert.'

He signals towards a chair. 'Then tell me about it.'

I sit. 'Robert was cheating with one of his colleagues. Her name is...was Leona.'

'Is,' the Professor clarifies. 'Leona is still alive and well, and we know all about the affair.'

I deflate. 'Then what was the point of sending me there.'

'You might notice something that the police didn't. How did Hudson feel? What was Robert's reaction?'

'He was worried, I guess.'

'Scared, you mean?'

'No, just worried that he'd screwed things up.'

'A fair assumption. And Martin? How did he react?'

I think back. At the time, the overriding emotion was anger. But now I consider it, that was one thread woven into a far more complicated tapestry. 'He was angry but also disappointed. And I think...'

'Go on.'

'I think he was frightened.'

'Of Robert? Impossible. Hudson held all the power. One phone call, one signature, and he could have destroyed him.'

I know this is true. I think of how I – Hudson – felt when he delivered his ultimatum. There was no question in his mind that he would be obeyed.

'Yes. But that's not what he wanted. He loved Robert like a son. Besides, Robert was his crutch. Every shortcut, every lapse in judgement, Robert was right by his side. You could say he knew where the bodies were buried. Metaphorically, of course.'

'So, you think he feared blackmail?'

'No.' I know I'm explaining it badly. 'Robert was useful to him. He didn't want to lose that relationship.'

The Professor narrowed his eyes. 'So now you don't think Hudson did it?'

I run my thumbnail along the wood grain on the edge of his desktop. 'I guess not.'

'No, it doesn't sound like it. Which is a small mercy; I wouldn't relish delivering a final summary to our client in which he's named as the culprit.'

'I can see why that wouldn't be ideal.' I'm already getting to my feet, keen for the humiliation to end.

As I reach the door, the Professor stops me.

'Your focus on feelings today was impressive.'

'But I didn't find any leads.'

'No, but your job is to observe and feel. We report it back to the family and their detectives. It's their job to use the information as they see fit.'

He doesn't say goodbye. I take the way he goes back to scribbling his notes as my dismissal and pull the door shut behind me.

Andrea isn't in the corridor where I expect her to be. I look both ways and see her staring through the glass panel in a door further down the corridor. Her arms are crossed over her chest and she is gnawing on her bottom lip. I don't like to see her so anxious.

'Hey,' I say, touching her arm.

She yelps and jumps away from me.

'I'm sorry. I didn't mean to scare you.'

I expect her to laugh at her overreaction. Instead, she studies me thoughtfully. 'It's fine.'

'What's wrong?'

She nods towards the window. The room is sound-proofed, masking the chaos. Inside is a man, strapped to a chair in the same way I was an hour ago. But that is where the similarity ends. He struggles against the bonds with such force that the veins in his neck are standing up. His jaw is clenched, and his teeth are bared so that I can see even the molars at the back of his mouth.

'What's wrong with him?'

'The medication.' The words seem to stick in Andrea's throat and come out strangled. 'A bad reaction.'

'That's an understatement.'

The white of the man's eyes are visible all around his

irises. They flit towards the door, and for a moment, I think he's looking right at me. 'Jesus! You know, I'm beginning to wonder if this is worth the money. Two jumpers in twenty-four hours ending up out of their minds; that can't be a good sign.'

'Maybe…I…' Andrea wraps her arms tighter around her as if she's trying to hold herself together.

'Hey, don't worry. He's in there, and I wouldn't let him hurt you. I'll look after you.'

She springs back again. 'No. I am nobody to you. Nobody. Do you understand me? I'll look after myself.'

'I'm sorry. I didn't mean to offend you. That must have sounded really misogynistic. But I like you. You're the only one around here that's nice to me.'

'I'm not your friend, Ryan. This is a job. Do you understand me? Nine to five, colleagues, nothing more.' She turns on her heel and storms away from me.

'Um, hello, technician, aren't you supposed to escort me?'

She doesn't answer.

I turn in a circle. I am alone.

Chapter Six

I'm sitting with my knees pulled to my chest when the door opens. I see Andrea peer at me through the crack. Then her hand appears, waving a white napkin.

'Truce?' she asks.

'Technically, I think you just surrendered.'

'Really? That doesn't sound like me.'

'No, it doesn't. What was all that about?'

She tosses the napkin onto the abandoned breakfast tray. 'I may have overreacted.'

'Just a bit. I was one step away from being pounded to dust.'

'Sorry. The other jumper made me nervous, and I took it out on you.' She fidgets with her ring, moving it up and down over her knuckle. An impressive looking diamond is clasped upon the band. It's clearly an engagement ring, but she wears it on her right hand. I wonder if this is the root of her tetchiness.

'I'm nothing like that guy. I think an existing violent streak is necessary to act like that, medication or not.'

Her tongue flicks over her lips. 'I doubt any of us know what we're capable of until we're pushed.'

'Well, I know myself, and I'm not capable of that.' It occurs to me how ridiculous that statement is; I don't know myself at all.

'Okay, I'm sorry. Let's just forget it. Do you want to go to the games room?'

'There's a games room?'

'Oh, yes. With everything your heart could desire. As long as that desire happens to be a chessboard with most of the pieces missing or table tennis without bats?'

'Stop it! It's like you're reading my mind right now.'

Andrea laughs, and I'm relieved the tension is beginning to lift. However, as we leave, she stops in her tracks, and her face darkens again. 'Ryan, did anybody see you come here?'

'Without my escort you mean? Don't worry, I kept out of sight.'

Her smile returns. 'Thank you.'

The games room is barely a minute's walk from my unit. The orderly from the canteen is the only person inside. He gives me a little salute before he goes back to his mopping. Other than him, we are alone.

This is no surprise; it is as glum as Andrea insinuated. The walls are painted an institutional green, and the windows are covered with a safety mesh.

I point to them. 'Now, is that to keep us in or to keep the looters out?'

'We have to protect these riches.' Andrea is searching

through a trunk of games. I hear the clatter of plastic. 'You didn't want to play Connect 4 anyway, did you?'

'No. I prefer to keep my undefeated title.'

She nods and returns the now empty box to the trunk. 'Aha!' She holds a pack of cards aloft. 'But I don't know if they're all here.'

I shrug. 'It might make things more interesting.'

The legs of the metal chairs shriek as we drag them up to the folding table.

Andrea clumsily shuffles the pack, shoving a few dropped cards into the middle. 'What shall we play?'

'I'm probably not the best person to decide. I don't remember the rules for any games.'

'Go Fish it is, then. We'll save Strip Poker for next time.' Her grin dissolves as soon as the words are out of her mouth. 'I'm sorry. That was really unprofessional.'

'It sounded like a joke to me.'

'No. Fifteen minutes ago, I was tearing you a new one over boundaries, and then I…It was inappropriate.'

'Hey, I won't tell anybody if you don't.'

She gives me a weak smile and begins to deal the cards. 'The aim of the game is to get as many sets of four cards as you can. You ask me if I have the card you're collecting. If I do, I hand it over. If I don't, I tell you to 'go fish' and you have to take a card from the pack.' She waves her hand at me. 'You'll pick it up as we go.'

'I'm sure I'll be fine.'

The orderly stops his work and squints to look at Andrea's cards over her shoulder. Then he holds his hand up to me, his thumb tucked against his palm.

I hide my grin behind my cards. 'Do you have any fours?'

She grumbles and hands me two cards. 'It's your go again.'

The orderly winks at me before he picks up his bucket and leaves.

'What are you smiling at?' Andrea asks.

'Just happy to be alive.' I decide to change the subject. 'You didn't ask me what happened in the jump. Any sevens?'

'Not my department. And go fish.'

I pick up a card.

She studies her hand. 'Any fives?'

I pass her a card and she celebrates with a cheesy fist pump.

'Isn't it part of your job to ask me about it?'

'Nope. I run the equipment and get you to where you need to be. The Professor deals with the rest of it. Any twos?'

'Go fish. Well, aren't you at least curious?'

'Not really. What card do you want?'

'Oh. Threes?'

'Go fish.' She bounces in her seat like a little kid.

I pick up a card. 'I'm afraid that gives me a set.' I lay my four cards face down on the table.

'Beginners luck!' She glances at her watch. 'I'm going to grab some water. Can I get you anything?'

'I'll have a glass, too.'

She lays down her cards. 'No peeking.'

'I don't need to cheat to win.'

'Well, I'm not sure those cards were even shuffled prop-erly,' she says over her shoulder.

'Excuses, excuses. Besides, you shuffled them!' I shout after her, but she has already disappeared.

I'm drumming my fingers on the top of my cards when Reynolds enters. He is followed by a blonde woman.

'Hello, Ryan. Do you mind if we ask you a few questions?'

'Sure.' I am looking at the woman, waiting for him to introduce us.

He doesn't. Instead, he drags one of the metal chairs over to the door and wedges it under the door handle.

'What's going on?'

He ignores my question.

The woman sits in Andrea's chair, and he pulls a seat up next to her.

'We would like to know what you saw on the jump today.'

'Okay. I've given all the details to the Professor. I'm sure he'll share the notes...'

'We prefer to hear it straight from you.'

'All right.' I look at the woman. She clutches her handbag on her lap like a security blanket. Foundation has settled into the wrinkles around her eyes. Still, they're a pretty shade of blue-green.

I must have been staring too long or something because she shifts in her chair. 'This is a mistake. I want to leave.'

'It's fine. Everything is fine.' Reynolds' hand is on her shoulder, stopping her from rising. 'Eyes on me, please, Ryan.'

'Sorry, I didn't mean to make you uncomfortable,' I say, but her head is bowed, and she is staring at the red leather of her bag. I turn to Reynolds. 'I learned nothing that we didn't already know. The affair, Hudson's warning; the Professor knew about it all.'

A whimper escapes the woman, forcing me to look at her again. That's when it hits me. 'You're Julia Hudson.' She was at least a decade younger in the jump, but the bird-like frame and sad eyes were the same.

I don't have time to say more before she's out of her seat and tugging at the chair keeping the door closed. 'Let me out! I want to go home!'

Reynolds opens the door for her. 'Okay, just wait outside. I'll only be a minute.'

Julia pushes past him before he can finish his sentence, and he returns to his seat. 'Losing her husband broke her.'

I cover my face with my hands. 'And I just told her he was having an affair.'

'She already knew that. Although, I'm sure she didn't appreciate being reminded.'

'A bit of warning would have been helpful. She looks a little different from in the jump.'

'That would have been about fifteen years ago.'

'Did she ever remarry?'

'No. Robert's body was never found so she wouldn't give up hope that he might come back. Also...' He hesitates. 'She had some bad experiences with a stalker. It left her with some trust issues.'

'I bet. Poor woman. Why did you bring her here?'

'She wanted to talk to you, for you to understand what all of this is for, why it has to be this way.'

'I get that. She wants me to see there are real people behind all of this. You can tell her I will do my best to help in any way I can.'

Reynolds is about to reply when Andrea throws open the

door. It hits the back of the chair that was wedged below it moments ago, and the crash makes me jump.

'What are you doing, Reynolds? We've been through this; only the Professor questions him. You don't know the damage you could cause.'

Reynolds raises his palms to her. 'He didn't know anything, anyway.'

Andrea flaps him towards the door. 'At this rate, you're going to get us both fired.' She slams the door behind him and then leans against it. 'Are you okay?'

'Babysitter, bodyguard – is there any job you can't do?'

She rolls her eyes. 'There's no job I can't fail at, apparently.'

Chapter Seven

Incubus. That's the first word to take shape through the haze of sleep. I pull the story from my subconscious like a thread you know it's a bad idea to tug at. A creature of mythology portrayed as a squat little demon that would sit on its victim's chest at night, preventing them from moving, terrorising them. Mythology, of course. Just ancient man's attempt to explain sleep paralysis. I'm not sure how I know this. Perhaps I've suffered nightmares such as these in my old life, because that's what this has to be, a bad dream. I'm not really pinned to my bed under the weight of a monster.

Seconds tick by before the realisation hits me with a sickening jolt. I'm not paralysed by the neurochemicals of sleep, and I'm not dreaming. Somebody is sitting on my chest.

'Pretty.' It's the man from the cafeteria. Lloyd, that was his name. He's straddling my chest, his knees holding my arms by my side. The skin of my cheek snags as he pulls something sharp across its surface. 'I'm going to make you beautiful.' He presses down and I feel white hot pain bloom on my flesh.

'Get off me.' I buck beneath him, but he tenses his thighs.

'Keep still. You are going to be a work of art.'

Hot liquid flows down my face. That's my blood. I tell myself this over and over, unable to grasp that it's actually happening. I twist my face away from him.

'Stop moving. You're ruining it!' Lloyd covers my face with flecks of spittle.

The door to my unit flies open and several security guards rush in. Two of them grab Lloyd's arms while a third smashes a baton down onto his wrist until he drops his weapon. A pair of scissors land on the bedspread next to me. Drops of blood drip onto the white linen. My blood.

He's still yelling as they drag him away. 'I haven't finished! Let me finish!'

One of the security guards hands me a handkerchief and I press it to my face. 'Are you okay?'

My mouth opens but I can't answer him. I have no words.

'Get up, and we'll take you to the infirmary.'

I do as I'm told, shuffling to the edge of the bed. When I try to put weight on my legs, they wobble and threaten to betray me. I'm on my feet when the world begins to spin. Then there is only black.

Chapter Eight

'They say we brought it on ourselves. But monsters are made, not born.' The voice penetrates the blackness that consumes me. 'So they need to take responsibility for that.'

'What are you talking about?' I try to sit up, but waves of nausea force me back onto the pillow. 'Who are you?'

'Nathan.' His tone is matter-of-fact, as though this should be obvious.

I blink until his silhouette begins to take shape. 'Oh, it's you.' The orderly from the games room stands over me. 'Nathan.' I roll the name around my mouth. It feels natural, familiar. 'Do we know one another? I'm sorry, I'm having some issues with my memory.' I push myself up onto my elbows.

'Now isn't the time to worry about that.' His fingertips make hot little circles on my chest as he pushes me back onto the pillow. 'Go to sleep.'

I sink back into the darkness.

When I surface again, someone is tugging up my eyelid and shining a light in my eye.

I slap the hand away. 'Get off me!' I scoot up the bed, rucking up the sheets as I go.

I'm in a hospital ward. A blue curtain is half pulled around me, offering privacy from one end of the long room.

On the other side, Nathan tucks sheets around an empty mattress. So he was here the first time I woke. Part of me believed it was a dream.

Andrea appears from behind the curtain. 'Calm down, Ryan. You're safe now.' She puts a hand on my shoulder but then pulls it away.

'How long have you been here?' I ask.

'A little while.' She turns to the doctor. 'Will he be okay?'

'He'll be fine.' He tucks the flashlight he's been using into his breast pocket. 'The wounds are superficial. But we'll keep him in tonight. I'll prescribe something for the pain.' The curtain billows as he passes it on his way out.

Andrea is frowning at me, and I wonder what I must look like to her, as I cower against the headboard of the hospital bed.

I force myself to unfurl my limbs and pull the blankets up over me. 'What happened to Lloyd?'

'You don't have to worry about him any more.'

'Oh really? Because the last time I saw him he was trying to turn me into a Picasso painting.'

'That never should have happened. He was supposed to be monitored at all times.'

'How did he get out? And into my room? It was locked when I went to sleep.'

'I don't know.' She massages her temples. 'But we're

going to find out. I promise.'

My hand goes to my cheek. 'What did he cut me with?'

'We think he stole a pair of scissors when they took him to the infirmary after his episode in the canteen.'

The skin around my wound feels tight. 'Did I need stitches?'

'Just a few,' the doctor says as he walks back towards my bed. 'You'll barely notice the scar.'

'Could I have a mirror please?'

Andrea and the doctor look at one another.

'Sorry,' Andrea says. 'That's against procedure.'

'I've just had my face sliced open, and you won't let me see the damage?'

Her brows knit. 'I would, but it's part of your contract. To jump into the hosts, you have to take on as much of their sense of self as possible. Not seeing your own image while you're here helps with that. There isn't even a mirror on the compound for me to give you.'

I try to think of one example I've seen since I've been here to contradict her. I can't.

'Believe me, you've still got your movie star good looks,' she says, patting me on the shoulder. She forces a laugh, but her eyes are wet with sympathy. 'I brought you some clean scrubs. Although, obviously, you are rocking the escaped mental patient look.'

Until now, I haven't noticed I'm wearing a hospital gown. I suppose they had to cut off my pyjamas.

'I'll see you in the morning.' Andrea's pulling on a suede jacket and it's only then that I realise she's wearing regular clothes, not her usual shapeless scrubs. Her hair is curled, and the vivid red creates a stark contrast with the black lace of her dress. I wonder where she has been, and who she was with. Maybe she was out with the man who bought her that ring.

I don't like to think of this, so I concentrate on picking the bobbles from the worn hospital blanket. 'Sure. If you've got to go, you've got to go.'

'I'll be back in a few hours.'

I shrug.

She doesn't reply, and when I look up, I am alone with the doctor. I don't know why this upsets me or why I expected her to stay.

'Ryan, are you listening to me?' The doctor is leaning over my bed.

'Sorry. What did you say?'

He hands me a plastic cup of water and some pills. 'Take these.'

Behind the doctor, Nathan waves a hand to get my attention. The shake of his head is almost imperceptible, and I might have missed it, but for the steely gaze and heavy frown that accompany it.

'Why?' I ask him. 'What are they?'

But it's the doctor who answers. 'It's just pain relief and something to help you to sleep.' He crosses his arms as he waits, making it apparent that the medication is not optional. I put the little cup to my mouth and tip the pills in. 'Good lad,' he says, clapping me on the shoulder.

When he turns away, I spit them into my hand. I look up to gauge Nathan's reaction, but he is nowhere to be seen.

'Get some rest,' the doctor says, pulling the curtain around the cubicle.

I stare at the ceiling and use my fingers to trace the arc of my wounds as I try to figure out how badly I am injured. The doctor's claim of a few stitches doesn't seem plausible. I tally the bumps of the sutures and count at least seven, maybe more, running like a train track from the corner of my eye to the point where my ear meets my jaw. Other, smaller cuts, branch from it.

I force my hands under the blanket and wedge them beneath my knees to restrain myself from further probing. My eyelids feel heavy as the adrenaline begins to leave my body, but the shuffling of footsteps makes it spike again.

The doctor's voice echoes around the infirmary. 'What are you doing?'

'Security,' an unseen man answers. 'The Professor said to keep an eye on him.'

'No need to worry about that. I just gave him a sedative strong enough to knock out a rhino. You should go get some sleep.'

I want to protest, to tell them that actually, I'd feel better with a guard posted on the ward. But I'm supposed to be slipping into an oblivious sleep and don't want to draw atten-tion to myself.

'If you're sure,' the guard says.

'I'm sure. He's going nowhere. What are they going to do with Lloyd?'

I long to hear the answer, but their voices drift off as they walk away from my bed.

I close my eyes, but Lloyd's face is tattooed on the back of my eyelids, with bared teeth and throbbing veins.

Pulling the blankets over my head does nothing but heighten the sense of claustrophobia pressing down on me. The air within the cubicle doesn't satisfy my lungs, no matter how many rasping breaths I drag in. Finally, I give up and toss the blankets aside.

Peering through the curtain, I see that nobody is around. The beds adjacent to and opposite my own are empty.

My hospital gown is tied loosely at the back, and the air conditioning sends a rash of goose pimples over my skin. I pull on the scrubs that Andrea brought, then slip through the curtain and out of the cubicle.

The cold from the tiled floor runs up through my body, and I hug my arms around me. Hearing no voices, I head for the corridor. I don't know where I'm going; I just know that I need to walk, to burn off some adrenaline and process what has happened to me. I peer through the windows into each of the locked rooms. Nothing but offices, each dimly lit with safety lights.

When I come to the last door, I notice that it isn't backlit like the others. I see something on the other side of the window move. I throw myself back against the opposite wall, my heart thumping in my ears.

When, after a few moments, I see nothing more, I take tentative steps towards the window and cup my hands around my face as I peer through the glass.

Once my eyes adjust, I see what looks like a lab. Tall cylinders of liquid are lit in an eerie blue. Floating within them are foetuses at every stage of development. Some are so small that it's impossible to decipher human features. Others have developed shapeless limbs and oversized heads. A trail of bubbles rises from the bottom of one of the cylinders.

As I strain to see what is towards the back of the room, I find myself looking into a pair of black eyes. A yelp escapes before I realise it's Nathan staring back at me.

The left side of his face is cross-hatched with pink scratches. Running through it is a jagged crimson slash, held together with blue thread.

No, it's not his face that has been deformed in this way; it's mine. The combination of the bright hallway and the dark room has turned the glass into a mirror, superimposing my wounds over his face.

My fingers trace the angry marks. I'm still counting the stitches when the pounding of footsteps echoes around me. I look at Nathan, but he is already retreating into the darkness of the lab.

'Put your hands up!' One of the security guards points a pistol at me. 'Now!'

I do as instructed. 'I was just taking a walk.'

The guard turns me to face the wall, pressing my face into the cool plaster. Then he pulls my arms behind my back. I feel the snap of a cuff around each wrist.

'Why are you doing this? I'm allowed to go for a walk, aren't I?'

He puts his mouth close to my ear. 'You gave up all your rights.' He spits in my face and I flinch as though I've been slapped.

The guard heaves me away from the wall and marches me back to my cubicle.

The doctor is waiting for us. 'Best we don't take any chances this time.' He stabs a needle into my arm.

The edges of the world begin to fray and blur. I try to blink the dancing spots from my vision but they multiply until I can see nothing else.

'Night night,' the guard says and shoves me backwards onto the bed.

Chapter Nine

The whispers come from every corner of the room, like unseen rodents scratching against the floorboards.

I push myself up, relieved to realise my hands are now uncuffed. 'Is someone there?'

'I'm always here.' Nathan steps from the gloom. His voice is low and gravelly.

'Oh, it's you. Did Andrea ask you to stay with me?'

He chuckles. 'No. But I can if you'd like.'

I nod my head, not caring if he thinks me immature.

'Okay then.' Nathan slides down the wall and sits on the floor in the corner beside the faux window.

I scan the room and pick out the familiar shadows of my unit. 'When did they move me here?'

The light from the window casts long shadows across his face. 'No idea. Although it makes no difference; same prison, different cell.'

'Prison? This is a job. At the end of the week, I get paid, and they won't see me for dust.'

Nathan huffs his contempt. 'In my experience, employers don't lock you in.'

My eyes dart to the door; I don't need to try it to know he's right. 'Yes, for our safety.'

'I see. How's that working out for you?'

Anger flashes through me. 'You know what, I don't need this right now. Take your conspiracy theories and your sarcasm and leave me alone.'

I roll over, dragging the covers with me.

'I'd love to,' he says to my back, 'but I'm just as trapped as you.'

'What do you mean?' I sit up too fast and my head swims. Pressing my face to my knees, I wait for the world to right itself.

When the spinning stops, I look to the corner but Nathan is gone; I didn't even hear him leave. I'm annoyed he didn't tell me he had a key. Not that I'd have gone with him. I need this job.

I must have fallen back into a restless sleep, because I wake with a start. The sheet is stuck to my wound and each millimetre I peel away brings fresh agony. Crimson droplets of blood join the crusted evidence of Lloyd's torture. This prompts a vision of him, teeth clenched into a deranged grimace, straddling my body.

I scurry from the bed, away from the scene of the crime. The blanket tangles around my feet and I drag it to the corner of the room with me.

Then I hear it. Andrea's voice manages to penetrate even the heavy fire door. Although muffled, the snap in her words is clear. I imagine her, fists balled by her side, jaw clenched, staring down her adversary. The image makes me strangely proud.

A key card beeps and the door opens. It is the way she freezes, her hand clasped over her mouth, that makes me turn away. I clearly look more of a mess than I did last night, and I don't want her to see me like this. Shame forces me back against the wall; I'd disappear through it if I could.

'You couldn't even be bothered to change the bedding?' She shouts this over her shoulder.

'Not in my job description,' I hear a man, I assume the guard, reply.

She goes back into the corridor. 'Maybe not, but it wouldn't hurt you to show a bit of humanity!'

A chuckle echoes from somewhere down the corridor. 'Perhaps you should tell him that.'

Andrea is muttering something under her breath when she crouches next to me. 'Ryan? It's okay. I'm here now.'

I bury my face in the blanket.

'Come on. Let me take a look. Please.'

I turn my head. If she feels the same blatant horror as before, she does a better job at masking it. Instead, she stares at my wound stony-faced, her anger betrayed only by the long exhale of breath through her nostrils. 'Right. Let's see what we can do here.'

She goes to the bathroom and comes back with a first aid kit I didn't know was there. As she rummages through it, it is clear that it contains little more than plasters and antiseptic.

'I can't believe they just left you like this.' She begins cleaning the traces of dry blood from around my jawline.

'The orderly came to check on me, but he didn't stay long.'

'Orderly?' The wipe has turned a dirty brown and she uses her teeth to tear open another.

'Yes, Nathan.'

Andrea freezes with the wipe poised above my wound. 'Nathan was here?'

'Yes. Is that a problem?'

'No, just...unexpected.'

The alcohol wipe brushes the stitches, and I wince.

'Are you going to be a baby about this?' she asks.

'I think I've earned a break.'

'I won't argue with that. There. Done. The doctor will be pleased his nice neat stitches survived. I think you just pulled them in your sleep.'

'Well, I was drugged.'

She collects together the discarded wrappers. 'What were you thinking? You never should have gone wandering off alone.'

'Yeah, well I thought that rule was for my safety. I didn't realise I was a prisoner.'

Nathan's words come back to me. My stomach twists when she doesn't immediately dismiss this accusation.

'It's just for a week. Then it will all be over.' She still hasn't met my eye.

'The guard spat in my face. He cuffed me.' Tears threaten, but I blink them back. 'What have I done to deserve that?'

Andrea grabs my hand. 'Listen to me. You have done nothing wrong.'

'Then why do the guards hate me so much?'

'They don't. Let me just wash my hands, and we'll decide what to do.' She gets up and heads for the bathroom. 'You know what I think it is?' she asks over the splashing of water. 'I think that guard got you mixed up with Lloyd. He's new and doesn't know anybody yet.'

'You think?'

'I do.' She reappears, drying her hands on a paper towel. 'Look, I'm going to tell the Professor that you aren't up to jumping today.'

'No, don't do that. If the alternative is staying locked up in here all day, I'd prefer to keep busy. As you said, one week and it's all over.'

The side of her mouth twitches, but she doesn't manage a smile. 'Exactly. You've got this.'

She waits outside as I dress.

I change quickly, desperate to get out of the unit, already dreading my return.

'There we are, good as new,' she says as I join her in the corridor.

I don't bother to respond.

'You'll be jumping into Luke Kennedy today.' Her voice is too bright, filling the silence between us with forced enthusiasm.

When we reach the lab, I take my place in the chair. As she gives the injection and I close my eyes, it occurs to me that it might be nice to be someone else for a while.

Jumping has become easier, as though my brain has learned to assimilate the information at a faster pace. When I open my eyes, I'm in a room lit by the idling screens of dozens of computers. The company name, 'Hudson & Bell', flits across the monitors.

I am more aware of the body I inhabit than I have been in previous jumps. Whereas before, I felt like little more than a stowaway, now it's as if I have shrugged on an ill-fitting suit. Still, when I try to manipulate the body I inhabit, Luke continues on his path undeterred.

A strange humming catches my attention and Luke walks us to a nearby office. He uses two fingers to prod the door open. It is only then that I notice it is his name inscribed on the plaque.

Relief washes through Luke and over me. 'Robert, you idiot. I thought we were being burgled.'

'No, just sorting some paperwork.' Robert walks forward, inserting himself between Luke and the piles of documents behind him.

'I see.' Luke sidesteps him. 'You're shredding all that? Why not put it in an incinerator bag? You'll be here for hours.'

'I wanted to look over it first. I've got a system going now.'

'Okay. Let me help you, then. Two of us will get it done much quicker.'

'It's fine...'

Luke has already snatched a file from the stack and is flicking through it.

It means nothing to me. The words and numbers dance around the page, as incomprehensible as a foreign language.

They mean something to Luke though. 'This is my account. Why are you shredding my files?'

'What? That must be a mistake.'

But Luke is already sifting through the pile. 'They're all mine.' His mouth is dry. 'What's going on?'

Robert runs his hands through his hair as he turns in a circle. 'I'm sorry. Hudson is on to us.'

Luke's stomach plummets. 'No. You said the amounts were too small, that nobody would notice a tiny slice of the interest.'

'Well, I guess I was wrong.' He feeds a page into the shredder.

Luke watches it disappear between the metallic jaws. Realisation washes over him in a cold wave. 'And now you're shredding every document with your signature on it, leaving just the computer files, which are stored in my password protected account.'

Robert says nothing but feeds another sheet into the machine.

All of a sudden, we're running towards him. Luke shoves him, and he falls backwards.

There is a dull thud as his head smacks the desk. When Robert pulls his hand away it is streaked with blood. He stares up, wide-eyed.

I open my mouth to apologise. But it isn't my mouth and Luke is in no mood for contrition. 'I'll tell Hudson everything. Maybe they'll let us share a prison cell.'

'Look, I have a plan. The money's safe. They'll never find it. And we can be gone before they even start looking for us.'

Luke's nerves are tingling with interest.

I want to stay longer, to listen, but already I can feel my consciousness being dragged back to my own body.

I squeeze my eyes shut against the glare of the lights above me.

'Luke and Robert were defrauding the company. They were in it together.'

'Save it for the Professor.' Andrea is undoing the Velcro from around my wrists.

'Don't you see how important that is? Luke had a motive.'

'Not my department.'

I push myself from the chair, exasperated by her lack of enthusiasm, and stalk towards the Professor's office.

'Robert and Luke were stealing from their clients.'

The Professor looks up at me from his paperwork. 'Please, come on in.' His tone is wry and laced with sarcasm.

I ignore it and sit down opposite him. 'When Hudson found out, Robert destroyed the evidence and made a plan to escape. Luke found him shredding the files so Robert offered to take him, too.'

'Did they say where?'

'Well, no. The jump was up by then.'

'Well, that's interesting information. You say he was shredding files?'

'That's right.'

'In his office?'

'Luke's office. Is that relevant?'

'Very. That was his last known location. We also found traces of his blood there.'

Realisation creeps over me. 'Luke pushed him, and he hit his head. But it was nothing really. He seemed fine.'

The Professor deflates. 'We thought perhaps that was where he was killed.'

'I can't rule it out. But Luke wasn't angry when I left. He was curious.'

'Today was useful.'

I know that is as close to a thank you as I'm going to get, so I head for the door.

'Could you send Andrea in?' he calls after me. 'I need a word.'

I wonder if I should sit back down and explain that she had nothing to do with my wandering last night. However, I decide it might get her into more trouble if it looks like we're too friendly, so I leave the office.

'He wants to talk to you.'

'What? Me? Why?' She smooths down the material of her un-ironed scrubs and fixes her ponytail.

It hasn't occurred to me before that I've never seen them together. I wonder if she's even met him.

'I feel like I've been called to the principal's office,' she says before she enters.

She is inside for far longer than I've ever been. I lean against the wall by the door, hoping to hear some of what is being said.

Without warning, the door flies open. Andrea's face is streaked with tears as she storms down the corridor.

'Where are you going?'

'Home.'

'But what about me?'

This stops her. She wipes her face with the back of her hand before she turns to me. 'I can't do this any more.'

'What do you mean? A few more days and it's over, remember?'

'I know. But you'll have to finish without me. I'll arrange a new technician for you. I'm sorry.'

Chapter Ten

The technician avoids looking at me. I, in comparison, scrutinise him as he glides around the lab. Slender fingers dance over the buttons on the console. Each movement is deliberate. Methodical. He certainly doesn't waste time on banter.

I miss Andrea already.

As he begins to attach the electrodes to my forehead, I grab his hand. 'What's your name?'

For a second, I think I see his eyes narrow, but then it passes. 'Sam.'

'It's nice to meet you, Sam.'

He moves onto the Velcro straps without returning the sentiment.

'Have you worked here long?' I ask.

'No.' He offers no further detail. 'Sharp scratch.' The needle pierces my bicep and the world fades.

When I open my eyes, I am standing at a sink. My eyes are drawn to the window. Julia's reflection stares back at me.

It occurs to me how small she is. Compared to her father, she is light, as though a stiff breeze could knock her over.

I'd like to study her face more closely, to take in the sweep of her jawline or the curve of her nose. But I know these are my observations, not hers. Julia doesn't want to look at herself, because she doesn't like what she sees. No, it goes beyond that. She's repulsed. I know, if she were to study her reflection, she would see gaunt hollows where I see elegant cheekbones. She would see dark circles where I see sparkling eyes. Her feelings threaten to overwhelm and choke me.

Instead, I force myself to focus on her actions. She is filling a glass under the tap. Water sloshes over the sides because her attention keeps flitting to the window. She tries to look away, but adrenaline won't let her.

Her fear sprouts and lays down roots in the pit of my stomach. The same thought echoes through both of our minds; somebody is outside.

Julia takes her water and flicks off the light switch.

A face looks back. A face I recognise. Warm breath has left a fog on the glass, but still, I see salt and pepper hair topping a bristled complexion.

The water glass crashes to the ground and Julia runs from the kitchen. Adrenaline has blunted her senses and she doesn't notice the figure in the dark hallway until she collides with him. When he grabs her arms, she pounds fists on his chest.

It is only when she notices his smell that she begins to calm down. She breathes in the rich oak of his aftershave.

'Robert, there was somebody outside the window.'

Robert lets out a sigh, laced with impatience. 'For God's

sake, not this again. You are really losing the plot, you know that?'

'I swear, someone was out there.' She says this with conviction but already I feel doubt creeping into her mind.

'And a man was following you in the car park yesterday. But did the cameras show anybody but you?'

His annoyance stings like a slap and she retreats within herself. 'No.' The word is barely a whisper.

'No. Yet we had police and security crawling all over that place at great expense.'

'I'm sorry.' She wants to cry, but she won't allow herself. It will only make him mad.

'Come here,' he says, folding her into his embrace. 'What are we going to do with you?'

I want to scream at him, to shake him, until he believes her. Because it wasn't just the fact that I saw him too that bothers me. It's that I recognised him, and for the life of me, I can't think of one good reason why Nathan would be standing outside Julia's window.

Chapter Eleven

'Welcome back,' Sam says.

It's my turn to dispense with the pleasantries. He has already released my arms, so I bound from the chair and make my way to the Professor's office.

Sam waits outside, arms crossed over his chest.

The office door opens before I can knock.

'Come in,' the Professor says. 'How was the jump?'

'Interesting. I saw Julia's stalker.'

'You did?' He taps his pen against his lower teeth. 'What did he look like?'

'I can do better than a description. I know his name. Professor, he works here.'

He stares at me. 'That's not possible.'

'It is. I saw him as clearly as you're sitting in front of me right now. His name is Nathan and he's an orderly here.'

'You're mistaken. There is no orderly called Nathan

working here.' The Professor gets to his feet and walks to the door. 'Sam, could you join us please?'

Sam takes a seat next to me. He fidgets in his chair, crossing an ankle over his knee before changing his mind and sitting with his hands in his lap.

'Do we have an orderly by the name of Nathan working in this facility?'

Sam shakes his head. 'Nobody by that name.'

'Then he gave me a fake name. But I'm telling you, I've met him.'

'Describe him to us,' Sam says.

'Greying hair, stubble, mid-forties.' I wrack my brain, wishing I'd paid more attention. 'I didn't imagine him. The man who killed Robert Lyle is here.'

The Professor's eyebrows raise. 'That may be the case, but there is nobody of that description on our staff.'

Chapter Twelve

They dump me back in my unit as soon as the Professor has finished with me.

I pace the length of the room, unable to settle. A shuffling from the other side of my door catches my attention. Probably the guard doing his rounds. But the footfalls stop right outside. I haven't seen Lloyd since the night he broke into my room. As far as I can tell, he's been removed from the facility. Still, I can't help but picture his grimacing face so close to the outside of my door that it makes damp little fog patches on its surface.

I scan the room for a weapon but find nothing. Instead, I grab the biggest book I can find from the shelf. I stand to the side of the doorframe, my copy of *War and Peace* brandished above my head, with every intention of smashing it down on his skull.

The lock clicks as somebody swipes a key card. My eyes are squeezed shut as I bring the book down.

A last-minute moment of hesitation makes me pull it up short and I peek through narrowed eyes.

Andrea cowers before me, the fawn folder she holds in front of her face her only protection. 'You were going to hit me.'

'Only because I thought you were Lloyd.'

I assume she believes me because she turns and closes the door. 'Give me that.' She takes the book from my hands and looks at the cover. 'What would Tolstoy say?'

'He'd probably be rolling in his grave.' The book thuds to the floor as I wrap her in my embrace. 'You came back.'

She is rigid in my arms. 'Well, I think I may have been a little melodramatic. It's only a couple of days.'

'Exactly.'

She wriggles away from my grasp. 'Besides, I was hoping to get your help with something.'

'Of course.' I realise I've agreed without hearing the task so, not wanting to sound too keen, I add, 'With what?'

'A delivery has come in down at the loading bay. I could use your help moving it.'

'The technicians do that, don't they?'

'We're Jacks of all trades. It's done at night so as not to disrupt the jump schedule. Tonight's my turn.'

'No problems.' A lightness spreads through me at the thought of being useful. I cram my feet into my plimsolls.

Andrea cracks the door and throws furtive glances left and right.

'What's wrong?'

'I'm not sure how the Professor would feel about this.'

'You haven't asked him?'

She twists the ring on her finger. 'No.'

'So this is an 'it's easier to ask for forgiveness than permission' kind of deal?'

Andrea smiles. 'Exactly.'

I follow her down the corridor. She stops at each corner, her index finger raised at me like an exclamation mark as she checks for guards.

'It's clear.' She tugs me towards an elevator and punches at the one button. Down.

The doors open onto a hallway lined with metal doors. Each one has a flap that can be taken down to view inside.

'Andrea, is this a prison?'

She ignores my question and continues to drag me towards the exit at the end.

I dig in my heels. 'Answer my question, or I'm not going any further.'

Andrea doesn't look at me. Her feet shuffle noiselessly on the grey linoleum as I wait for her to respond.

When she turns, she hugs the folder to her chest. 'It's just a precaution. You experienced it first hand with Lloyd. They need somewhere to keep the jumpers if they lose control.'

Her answer makes perfect sense. It sounds sensible even. But there is something in the way she chews at the side of her mouth, lips pursed, that tells me it's not the whole truth.

I go to tell her as much, but the whir of the lift interrupts me. Before the doors open, Andrea shoves me into one of the open cells. She holds her finger to her lips, as though I'd have any intention of making a noise and getting her into trouble.

The flap is open, and together we watch three men walk down the corridor in single file, flanked by two security guards. The first chats with the guard next to him but the other two follow in silence. The door to the cell opposite squeaks as they open it.

'Here we go.' The first man bounces on the balls of his feet, as though adrenaline is forcing him into perpetual motion.

I glance at Andrea but she is staring ahead.

'I don't think I can do this,' says the man at the back of the line. He steps back towards the lift.

'Are you serious? How long have we waited for this?' I see a flash of wood as the first man brandishes something in his hand.

'I'm sorry; I just can't.'

'After what he did?' The first man's lip jumps up in a snarl of disgust. 'Then wait out here.'

After unlocking the door, the guards take up their stations on either side.

The two remaining men head into the cell, pulling the door closed with a metallic thud. Despite this, I can still hear muffled voices from within. Although I can't tell what they're saying, the slight raise in intonation at the end of each sentence tells me they are questioning whoever is inside.

Then the talking stops, and the shouting starts. A scream pierces the air, guttural and stretched, punctuated only with the thwack of what I assume is wood on flesh.

The third man crouches on the floor, his hands clasped over his ears. When I look over at Andrea, she is slumped in the corner, her face buried in her knees.

But I can't look away. No, more than that. I don't want to. It feels only right to bear witness.

It lasts just minutes. A frantic banging comes from within and the guards open the door.

A figure launches into the corridor. Doubled over, the man who had been so excited to get into the cell now vomits onto the faded linoleum.

His friend follows him out and clasps his shoulder. 'Was it everything you hoped for?' His voice is flat and he heads for the lift without further comment. The guards lock the door and the group file after him.

When we hear the lift doors close, Andrea peeks into the corridor. 'Come on.' She heads straight for a door at the end of the corridor.

I don't follow her. Like a magnet, I am drawn to the cell opposite.

'Ryan, leave it,' she hisses.

The flap falls open with a clink.

Lloyd is sprawled on the floor. His fingers have made bloody trails where he must have tried to crawl away from his assailants. Despite his dark curls, I can see the way his hair is matted and slicked. The skull beneath is misshapen, his forehead ending abruptly above his eyebrow. A baseball bat lies half under the bed, as though hiding from its role in this crime.

My hand flies to my mouth as I suppress the urge to wretch. 'Jesus, what have they done to him?'

Andrea stands with her back to me, refusing to look. 'What a lot of people would have liked to. Don't you agree?'

My fingers instinctively go to the slashes on my face. Sure, I've thought about revenge, my fantasies even straying into violence. Although I like to think I am above it, what would I have done if they'd opened the door I hid behind and handed me a bat? I couldn't, hand on heart, say I wouldn't have accepted.

Chapter Thirteen

‘You knew. You knew they were going to kill him.’ I long for her to deny it.

Instead, she refuses to look at me. A muscle in her jaw tics. ‘Look, I promise, I will explain everything, but we have to go.’

‘Or what?’

She doesn’t answer so I do so for her. ‘Or I end up like him.’

Her ‘yes’ is barely audible. For the first time, her eyes meet mine and they are brimming with tears. ‘I’m sorry.’

‘Sorry? You expect me to fall for this act? You’re as much of a monster as them.’

‘I know.’ Her tears leave jagged mascara tracks on her cheeks. ‘So let me do what I can to fix it.’

‘The lift is rumbling again and she stares at it, wide-eyed and unblinking. ‘Please, come with me now, or I’ll have to leave you here.’

My desire to survive overrides my disgust, and I nod.

Andrea heads for the security door and swipes her key card. She is easing it closed just as the lift opens.

The room in which we hide is shrouded in shadows with the only source of light coming through the frosted door panel. Two trollies have been abandoned at the back of the room, their cargo covered by white sheets.

We stand on either side of the door. Andrea clasps her hand over her mouth, as though she doesn't trust herself not to betray us.

Two figures move behind the clouded window, each just a smudge of colour. The squeak of trolley wheels is followed by a voice tinged with irritation. 'Great; he's still alive.'

'Well, you'd better make yourself comfortable then. We'll have to wait him out.'

'My shift is over in half an hour. Look, he's going to the incinerator anyway. Does it really matter?'

A gasp escapes Andrea, mirroring my own horror, as we realise they are debating burning a person alive.

His companion laughs. 'Man, that is cold! No less than he deserves, I suppose. But I'm afraid there's a special request from the victim's family; he's going to be an organ donor.'

'Awesome. That's my plans ruined then.'

My body slumps in relief. They won't be wheeling Lloyd into this room anytime soon. For now, we are safe.

Andrea doesn't pause for celebration. She is pointing to a door on the opposite side of the room. She moves in an arc past the two trollies, as if even entering the space around them feels dangerous to her.

In contrast, I am drawn to them. My hand lingers over the shape on the trolley as I pass. Before I make a conscious decision to do so, the zip is in my hand and I am revealing the face below.

A bag has been taped around his neck, cutting off his air supply. I am sure that if I were to let the zipper continue around the corpse, it would reveal hands bound in the same way. The mouth is open, plastic sucked within as if the victim was making one last desperate attempt to breathe. His final emotions are etched on his face. I don't see rage in his eyes, or even fear, just confusion and a question – Why?

My mouth falls open in sympathy, and a strangled cry escapes. 'How can they get away with this? Doesn't anybody miss these people?'

'You can't miss someone who never existed. Now please, Ryan, come on.' Andrea drags me through the door into another room. A large machine stands in the middle. A chimney leads to the ceiling, so I assume it's the incinerator. It doesn't look like the massive oven I expected. Instead, it looks like the metal drawer of a filing cabinet. Pull it out, pop your secrets inside, and send them to oblivion.

Andrea is already standing by the huge shutter that blocks our path to the outside world. 'Will you hurry up.' I'm unsure whether she is talking to me, or the loading door that is inching up in front of us. 'It's best we draw as little attention as possible. So when it gets to waist height, I'm going to close it again. We need to get under before it crushes us.'

'Then what?'

'Then you run for the fence and haul your skinny butt over it as quick as you can. My car is parked on the other side, behind those trees.'

I'm at a loss for words so I give a simple, 'Okay.'

My heart beats in my chest as I watch the sluggish door fold in front of me.

Andrea kneels to look underneath. Satisfied that the coast is clear, she yells at me, 'Go!'

The freezing concrete shocks me as I roll across the floor. I pull in a lungful of fresh air as the cavernous ceiling of the crematorium is replaced with a cloudy sky.

I scramble to my feet and help Andrea do the same. She's already running. 'This way.'

As we reach the chain link fence, I launch myself at it, jamming my shoes into the gaps. My plimsolls are not made for climbing, so my arms are forced to carry most of my weight. Andrea is already at the bottom on the other side when I swing my leg over the top.

My burning biceps sing with relief as I allow myself to drop to the pavement. Pain shoots up my calves, but Andrea allows me no time to recover.

'Move.' She scrambles for the trees, and I follow without question.

Chapter Fourteen

ndrea swipes fast food containers from her passenger seat, and I sit with my white, hospital issue plimsolls covered by them.

'Sorry,' she says. 'I didn't think to...'

'No worries.' These pleasantries feel ridiculous considering the context; she's just helped me escape some malevolent agency. They might have already discovered I'm missing and be on their way to bring me back. Considering this possibility, I decide to be blunt. 'What did you mean when you said Lloyd wasn't alive? He felt very real when he was slicing my face open.'

'That's not what I said. He was real, all right. I said he didn't exist. Not on paper at least. He doesn't have the documents that society demands to be considered a bona fide living person.'

'They destroyed them?'

'No.' She goes quiet, and I'm not sure if it's because she's navigating a junction or because she's considering her answer. 'He never had any paperwork.'

'Then, what, he was an illegal immigrant?'

'No. He wasn't registered here or anywhere.'

'I find that hard to believe. Nobody can build a life nowadays without leaving some kind of paper trail.'

'You can if you're only a week old.'

I blink at her wordlessly for so long that she waves a hand in front of my face.

'Ryan? Did you hear what I said?'

'Yeah. You said that the fifteen stone man that attacked me was a newborn.'

'Only in terms of time. Physically he was in his twenties.'

'Right. So he's some kind of genetically engineered person?'

'Not some kind. A very specific kind. He's a clone of Marcus Steven Lloyd.' She's staring at me as if awaiting my response.

'Should that mean something to me?'

'I guess not. Lloyd was one of the most infamous serial killers of our era. He mutilated and murdered fifteen women over six months.

I think back to his promise to make me into a work of art and realise that I've experienced his mutilation first hand. 'Jesus Christ. Why would they want to bring someone like that back?'

'It's different in each case. Sometimes the families need to know why. They didn't get the answers they wanted while the original was alive. But often it's just a matter of revenge. Those men who beat Lloyd to death were the family of one of his victims. They are very rich and very angry.'

I pictured the man huddled in the hall, his comrade vomiting nearby. *Was it everything you hoped for?* That was what their friend asked. Now I think I would like to have heard his answer.

'But he wasn't guilty of those crimes. It was...' What word was it she used? 'The original.'

She gave me a sideways glance. Then she flipped down the sun visor above my seat.

'Look in the mirror and tell me he was innocent.'

My cuts have begun to scab over but they are still puckered and angry. I flip up the visor, unable to look at my reflection any more.

'I'm not saying that. But if the state put the original to death, how can he be carrying on...' I swallow hard. '...his work?'

'Memory is stored in DNA. It would be just as valid to ask me how he could talk, how he could read. Murder seems to be a learned 'skill' and is encoded there like anything else.' She takes her hands from the wheel as she adds air quotes to the word skill.

'Do you mind?' I say, nodding towards the steering wheel. 'I'm feeling nauseous enough as it is.'

'Sorry.' She places a hand back on it. 'One week. That's all we get before the memories surface and the clone's full character returns. They tried manipulating every variable they could think of. Age, nutrition, environment; they tried changing them all, and seven days was the best they could manage.'

'What does it matter? If they're going to interrogate them, don't they want them to remember?'

'The hope is we can manipulate them before that

happens. Get them to feel some empathy for their victims and their families. It makes it more likely they'll answer the questions the family want.'

'Okay. So where do the jumpers come into all this?'

The car swerves, and for the first time she puts both hands on the wheel. 'Excuse me?'

'The jumpers? Where do we fit?'

She presses her lips together so hard that they lose all colour. 'Ryan, I thought you understood. There are no jumpers. There are only technicians and...'

My stomach knots, and bile stings my throat. 'And clones.'

Chapter Fifteen

I am falling. I have been since that word slipped from my tongue, fracturing my world. Clone. A copy. An echo of a real person.

'Are you okay?' Andrea asks. 'That's a pretty stupid question, I guess.'

We walked from the car, up a stairway that stank of damp carpet, and into her flat without uttering a single word. Or at least I did. I have a vague notion that Andrea has asked me this question before and has been waiting for me to answer.

I don't. Instead, I give her a look that I hope is withering, that makes her feel as small as I do. I know it isn't her fault; don't shoot the messenger and all that. But how can I possibly be 'okay'?

'Please talk to me.' She gets up from the sofa and heads to the kitchen, if it can be called that. It is really just a corner of the same room with a sink and worktops crammed in. 'I know this is a lot to process. You were never supposed to find out.' She opens cupboards and closes them again, muttering something under her breath. 'Aha,' she says, pulling out a box of tea bags.

'You don't live here?' I ask as I see her search the drawers for a spoon.

'No, they'll be looking for us at mine. This place belongs to...a friend.'

Jealousy bubbles within me, and I will it to quiet. Even if this place belongs to the man who gave her that ring, it's none of my business.

She flicks on the kettle. 'If it makes you feel any better, I think you're innocent. I mean your original was.'

Innocent? My brain hasn't even started to process that part yet, as though it has an independent will and is allowing me only a certain amount of trauma at a time. 'My original was a serial killer?'

She is quiet as she pours the water. 'I don't know. I don't know anything about him.'

'You knew about Lloyd, and you weren't even his technician.'

'Everybody knew about Lloyd, but not through the agency. He was in every newspaper in every country at one point. I only started last week, so I knew they wouldn't allocate me him. But still, he gave me the creeps.'

It is a small consolation to hear that I was not infamous enough for her to have heard of me. But still, if I am guilty, we are talking shades of grey. Murder is murder.

'They must have told you something about me.'

'No. It's too risky. They don't tell the technicians anything. We could accidentally let something slip. That could trigger memories and...'

'And you could have a deranged killer on your hands.'

Andrea sighs. 'As I said, I'm not even sure you're guilty.'

'You can't know that.'

'You're right. It's just a feeling.' Her eyes flit to the file she discarded on the coffee table. 'I took that from the Professor's office before I came for you.'

'It's about me?'

She nods. 'I haven't looked. It didn't seem right.'

'That isn't smart. I might make Lloyd look like a choir boy.'

'I'm an optimist. Besides, they give the dangerous ones to the more experienced technicians. The guy Lloyd attacked in the canteen trained me. They can't risk a newbie screwing up.' She hands the file to me. We freeze with it held between us.

'Why are you helping me? You'll be in trouble for this, and considering what these people are capable of, I imagine losing your job will be the least of your problems.'

'I like an underdog. And the way they treated you was appalling.'

'You mean at the hospital?'

'And before.' She hands me my tea and then stares into her own cup. 'You know they did that on purpose, don't you? They let Lloyd out to see what he would do.'

'They used me as bait?'

'You aren't a person to them. They created you for a purpose, and they get to decide what that is. The Professor told me that they wanted to see what Lloyd would do without his usual 'type' to hand.'

'Well, it appears he will – would – make do with whatever flesh is available.' I'm still not sure how I feel about his death. The slash on my face radiates heat, reminding me of what he did to me.

I flick through the folder. On the first page is a picture I recognise. Hair peppered with grey. A permanent frown betrayed by a deep crease between the eyes. My hand goes to my brow. It's me, but much older. 'I've seen him... me...before.'

She leans over my shoulder. 'Where?'

'Outside Julia's kitchen window. I think my original was her stalker.' I flip to the page with my biography. 'It can't be true.' But there it is in black and white. Nathan Alexander Ryan.

Chapter Sixteen

I stare at the page. Nathan Alexander Ryan. 'They gave me my surname as a first name,' I say. 'Just like Lloyd.'

'Yeah, they do that with all the...They do it with you all. It helps you accept the cover story. They found in the initial trials that if a clone was given a completely different name to the original, they rejected it and the memories came back instantaneously. The same if you called them by their given name. But calling them by a name with a grain of truth in it, like their surname or middle name, created the right amount of confusion to stop their past from surfacing.' Andrea's eyes are bright as she tells me this, a magician revealing a trick, and for the first time, I question her role. She has been one of them, a cog in the machine designed to manipulate people like me.

I think she senses my disgust, because she changes the subject. 'You know, just because you were at the Hudson-Lyle house, doesn't mean you killed anyone.' But I watch doubt fog her features and know she isn't convinced by her own words.

'Do you actually believe that?' I reached out to turn the page and accidentally brush her hand.

Andrea flinches away. 'I'm sorry. Don't take it personally. I'm a little jumpy is all.'

'That's understandable.'

'Give me ten minutes, okay? I need to clear my head.' She disappears into the bedroom, leaving me to look through the file alone. The sound of water tells me she is in the shower.

The file states that Lydia and James were the names of my parents, as the Professor told me. He left out the fact that they died in a house fire when I was just a teenager. Perhaps this shaped me, nurtured the violent streak that must run through me like a stick of rock.

The next page has one word printed on it in stark block capitals: CONVICTIONS.

I get up and pace from one side of the tiny room to the other. I'm not sure I want to turn the page.

'It's all in the past, you know.' Andrea stands at the door to the bedroom, towel drying her hair. I notice some of the red dye has bled onto the white material and wonder what our host will say. 'What's inside that file, I mean; you can't change it. So whether you look or not, it's still there.'

'If you're trying to be reassuring, you're failing miserably.' I flip over the page.

Victim: Robert Lyle

Location of body: Unknown

Sites of interest: Hudson & Bell Enterprise. Blood was found at the scene. Signs of a struggle.

I stop reading. 'It says they never found a body. Just a bit of blood in the office. And I know from the...' I feel foolish saying it but there is no other way to describe it. '...from the jump that he was fine; he just had a little cut.'

'What are you saying?'

'What if he's not dead at all? What if I...Nathan was wrongly convicted?'

Her eyes search the worn carpet. 'I don't know, Ryan. If they had no body, surely there must have been other evidence. They don't just put a man to death with no evidence.'

My throat constricts and the room spins. An image crashes into my consciousness. A lamp is shining in my eyes. I want to squeeze them shut, but I know I can't. My arms are strapped to the bed. I arch my neck and try to catch one last glimpse of her. My love. My everything. Julia.

'Ryan?' Andrea is passing me a tumbler of water. 'Drink this. Did you remember something?'

'My death. It was by injection.'

'I'm sorry.' She reaches over to take the folder, trailing her index finger down the page as she reads. 'I think it's a pretty safe bet that Robert Lyle is dead.'

'Why's that?'

She turns the page to me and stabs a finger towards the bottom. 'You confessed to killing him.'

Chapter Seventeen

'Nathan. Nathan confessed,' I correct. I take the folder from her. It's there in black and white. Apparently, he handed himself in but refused to tell them how or why he'd done it. 'But why would he do that and then not tell them where the body was?'

'Guilt, perhaps. He couldn't live with what he'd done.'

'I'm not sure I could do the same in that position. But then it's not something I can even imagine doing, whether we're genetically identical or not.'

'His fingerprints were all over their home, the office, and both Julia's and Robert's cars. Maybe he thought it was just a matter of time before he was caught anyway.'

'It doesn't seem enough to force a confession. For stalking, maybe. But murder?' The likelihood that I am guilty seems to multiply as we speak. We sit in silence, both staring at the folder as though it could explode.

'Maybe that's exactly what happened, a forced confession,' Andrea says. 'Perhaps Nathan was pressured into admitting to something he didn't do.'

My chest loosens a little at this possibility. 'That feels right. I think that might be what happened.'

'Okay. Now we just have to find a way to prove it.' She goes to the window and pulls the curtain aside. 'The sun's up. Maybe we should pay Julia a visit. Is her address in the file?'

'No, but it doesn't matter. I know where she lives.'

Andrea's eyebrows jump up but she does not comment.

'Or I did anyway. She might have moved.'

'Well, it's the only lead we have, so we have to try.'

Directions pop into my head as Andrea drives us through the city. I don't question them and neither does she; we both know that Nathan's memories are guiding us. We've left early enough to avoid the morning rush, but Andrea still curses each time we get stuck behind a slow driver or hit a red light.

'Do you have any idea what you're going to say to her?' she asks.

I've been thinking about nothing else, but still, my answer is, 'No.'

'Because we can't just walk up and knock on her door. The Hudsons are billionaires; they'll have security.'

'I'm open to ideas.'

We drive the rest of the way in silence.

'That's it,' I say, pointing to a large house, clad in black wood. A wall of glass catches the reflection of the tree-lined street.

'Yeah, figures. Biggest house on the block.' Andrea turns

off the engine. 'What now?' She doesn't have to wait long for her answer.

Julia emerges through the front door, rummaging in her handbag. She doesn't see me walk up to her.

'Julia, please don't be frightened. I just need to ask you a few questions.' Palms spread, I approach her as though she is a baby deer, ready to bolt.

Her eyes widen with recognition. 'No.' Her voice is a whisper. She says it again, this time her voice tinged with anger. 'No. You can't be here.'

I expect her to run, like some stumbling heroine in a horror film, dropping her keys as she heads for the door.

Instead, she turns on her heel. 'Get out of here before I call the police.'

Andrea steps out from behind a tree, into Julia's path. 'If you want answers, you'll talk to him.'

She is pale but she juts out her chin in defiance. 'Fine.'

Chapter Eighteen

'They let you walk those things now?' Julia talks to Andrea over my head. 'I thought they were supposed to stay locked up.'

'We've been known to make the odd exception if we think it will produce results.' This lie rolls naturally from Andrea's tongue, which makes me wonder if there is any truth to it. The thought of the likes of Lloyd being set free in the world, no matter the reason, gives me chills.

'Well, keep him on a short leash. Nobody else should get hurt.'

Although I can't remember her, fondness bubbles to the surface when I look at Julia. It is at odds with the cruel words directed at me. This isn't the woman Nathan knew. Her edges have hardened. Or maybe she was always like that but her thorns were cloaked by his feelings for her.

'I'm sorry if my original hurt you.'

Her eyes dart to Andrea. 'He knows?'

'His memory came back quicker than expected. But we've found him amiable.'

Julia lets out a little snort. 'Amiable? He's an animal and deserves a bullet for what he did to Robert.'

I could point out the distinction between myself and Nathan, but I know her anger would blind her to reason.

'Nathan Ryan was executed for that crime,' Andrea says. I could hug her. 'Our goal here is to find out what he did with Robert's body.'

Julia folds her hands into her lap and slumps, chastised. 'What is it you want?'

Andrea glances at me, and I realise neither of us has any idea. 'Tell us about the day he went missing.'

'I've been over this a thousand times, but fine. We'd quarrelled the day before. He had been angry at me for wasting money with my paranoia over being stalked.' She lets out a tinny laugh that contains no humour. 'The next morning he apologised for snapping. He said he was just concerned, and we'd sit down and discuss it properly over dinner that evening. But he rang during the day and told me he had to work late. I never saw him again.' She looks pointedly at me.

'And Luke Kennedy confirms he was at work that day?' Andrea asks.

'He...Yes, I believe he did.'

I grasp at this straw. 'You don't appear so sure about that.'

Bitterness leaks from her pores. 'If I don't seem sure it's because I don't want to answer for a dead man. Luke killed himself shortly after Robert went missing.'

I think back to Luke's horror at Robert's betrayal. With Robert gone, the guilt of their actions would have weighed on his shoulders alone.

'I'm sorry to hear that,' Andrea says. 'Do you know why? Did he leave a note?'

Julia hesitates. 'No. He didn't leave a note.'

'You don't think it had anything to do with his business irregularities then?' I ask.

She glares at me. 'I couldn't possibly speculate.'

'I'll be blunt,' Andrea says. We know Robert was willing to let Luke take the blame for the fraud they were both guilty of. Perhaps that was motive enough to kill him?'

Julia huffs. 'Luke knew what he was doing. It might have been convenient for him to play the overgrown child, but he did very well out of that arrangement. Look, I really have nothing else to add.'

Andrea stands to leave. 'Thank you for your time.' She throws me a questioning look when I don't get up.

'Julia...' I say.

'Mrs Lyle.'

'Sorry. Mrs Lyle. I was wondering...' Already I regret starting this question, but I can't go without asking. 'Did you know Nathan at all? Even just in passing?'

The details of our relationship lie just beyond the periphery of my memory, but in other ways she's familiar. I know she covers her mouth when she laughs, that she hates the taste of alcohol, and that morning is her favourite part of the day. These seem too personal to have been learned peeping through a window.

I'm still seated but she stands and looms over me. 'The first time I ever spoke to him was at his trial when I told him to rot in hell.' She walks to the door and pulls it open. 'Now if you'll excuse me, I have things to do.'

I pause on the doorstep. 'You said Nathan deserved a

bullet for what he did. Is that how you would have done it if you got to kill him personally? A gun?'

Really, I would like to ask what they had planned, once they'd got all the information they could from me. How did they want me to die?

She frowns. 'No, I'd have chosen something long and painful. Because that's the life he left me with when he refused to tell us what he did with Robert.'

Chapter Nineteen

'What now?' I ask as we climb back into Andrea's beaten-up Citroen.

'I don't know. I didn't exactly plan this, you know. Not past getting you out of the facility, anyway.'

'I know.' As I cover her hand with mine, she pulls it away and starts the engine.

'Well, we can't drive in circles forever.'

'We could try Martin Hudson next,' I suggest, staring out of the window so she won't see the sting her rejection has caused. 'Maybe it will give his address in the file.'

'Are you sure you want to? After all, he was the person who—'

'Shhh,' I say, holding up a finger to her. 'I'm trying to forget that he paid for the privilege of killing me.'

'Charming,' she says, though she does as I ask. 'But there's no need to check the file. Hudson isn't at home.'

'How would you know?'

'Well, when one of the wealthiest men in Georgia, probably the country, has a heart attack, the news tends to report it.'

'Is he alive?' My motives for asking are selfish. It would be just my luck for him to die and take some crucial evidence with him.

'Apparently. His family press release says he's doing well and is recovering at the Savannah General Hospital.'

I relax a little. 'Okay. Let's go there then.'

The streets around us begin to take on a strange familiarity. It's an odd sensation, as though I recognise them from a film. 'I think Nathan was here.'

She cranes her neck to read a street sign. 'Harper Street. I didn't see it in the file.'

'Turn here.' On reflex, I put my hand on the wheel, and she slaps it away.

'Are you insane?'

'Please, I need you to stop.' I open the car door before we've even finished moving.

'Ryan, wait for me.'

When she catches up with me, I am standing outside a shop with a red neon sign. 'I know this place.'

'I bet you do.'

It's only then I realise it's adults only.

'Not this shop specifically...' I try to backtrack and then dismiss her with a wave when she starts to laugh at my discomfort.

I head for the alley down the side of the building. Split garbage bags have vomited their insides over the pavement. Despite the cold weather, the smell assaults my nose.

Andrea grimaces in disgust. 'There's nothing down here, Nathan.'

'I'm sure...' I turn in circles, hoping for something to trigger my memory. 'Over there.'

I lead her to a set of concrete steps, hidden from view by a dumpster.

'What's down there?'

I ignore her question, mainly because I have no idea, and rap my knuckles hard on the door at the bottom.

The man who opens it stares at me wordlessly. Finally, he sighs. 'Can I help you?'

'I hope so. Do you know me?'

His eyes narrow. 'Go back to your halfway house. Damn crackheads.'

He tries to pull the door closed but I grab it before he can. 'Please, do I look familiar?'

'What's going on?' A woman's voice comes from the space behind him. The man pushes the door wider to reveal her. Her features are as angular as the lines of the pantsuit she wears. When she looks at me, her frown dissolves into slack-jawed shock. 'Nathan?' She takes a step back. 'It's impossible.'

'You know me?'

'Of course I know you. Knew you. You're dead.'

'The rumours were exaggerated,' I say, spreading my arms wide.

'Well, I guess you better come in.' She turns to the security guard. 'Radio ahead and tell them I am bringing up Nathan Ryan.'

'Her too.' I point towards Andrea, who stands with her arms wrapped against the cold at the top of the stairs.

The guard looks at the woman, and she gives a near imperceptible nod.

I am led down another staircase into what I now realise is a club. The stage is lit with a floodlight, despite the lack of performers.

A man stands as I approach. 'I thought Erin must have been hallucinating. Nathan Ryan. I said it at the time, didn't I, Erin? There is no way they ever took down Nathan Ryan.' He holds my hand for longer than necessary, taking the opportunity to study my features past my bandages. 'Had some work done, I see.'

'Something like that.'

'And who is your lovely friend?' His eyes travel up and down Andrea's body.

Irritation gnaws at my nerves. 'She's none of your business.'

His eyebrows shoot up in shock. 'I see they removed your sense of humour along with your wrinkles.'

Andrea leans forward and offers him her hand. 'I am quite capable of talking for myself. Hi, I'm Andrea.'

He cups it with his own bear-like hands. 'At least somebody has remembered their manners. It's a pleasure, Andrea. I'm William.' He points towards the seat opposite and we both sit down.

'Can I get either of you a drink?' We shake our heads so he continues. 'Well, if we're disposing of the pleasantries, then let's get to business. I assume you are here for your usual?'

I decide to take a gamble and tell him, 'Yes.'

'Okay then.' He nods at Erin, who has been leaning on a pillar behind us. She disappears into a door marked 'office'.

We are left in awkward silence, although William's grin doesn't fade for a second.

Erin returns and hands him a small black bag.

'You realise the price has gone up. Inflation, you understand.' He pushes the bag over to me. 'Besides, you're a known criminal now.'

My palm rests on the bag. 'I'm sorry, but I don't have any money.'

For the first time, William's smile dims, but it returns moments later. 'I suppose I can extend a little credit for an old friend. As long as you settle up as soon as your 'business' is concluded.' He uses his fingers to put quotation marks around the word business.

'Much appreciated.' As I get to my feet, I take a peek inside the bag. It contains a gun.

Chapter Twenty

'Why would he think you want a gun?' Andrea hasn't spoken since we left the club, but now her tone is loaded with accusations.

'How am I supposed to know? I'm not Nathan, remember?'

I wait for her to agree, but she just chews at the skin around her thumbnail.

'Look, let's just stick to the plan,' I say. 'We'll go to the hospital and see if Hudson can tell us anything useful.'

Andrea still doesn't respond but turns the car in the direction of the Savannah General. When we arrive, she wastes no time getting out.

I linger for a moment, taking the opportunity to stick the gun into the waistband of my jeans. If William and his cronies are a reflection of the circles Nathan moves in, I intend to keep it close.

We make our way up to the cardiac ward with no issues. The lift doors ping open and we step into the brightly lit corridor. It brings back memories of the facility, and I shudder.

'Shall we ask at the reception desk which room he's in?'

Andrea jabs a finger towards the corridor to our right. 'I'm going to wager a guess that his is the one with the security guards posted outside.'

The men don't even acknowledge us as we approach.

'We're here to visit Martin Hudson,' Andrea says.

No response.

'We're old friends,' I add.

The guard's eyes flit to me. 'No visitors.'

I am considering our next move when the door behind him opens. Edith Hudson stands frozen within the frame. I brace myself for her scream.

Instead, she straightens up, her head high. 'I guess you'd better come in.'

We follow her into the room. Machines beep a regular rhythm. Tubes snake around Martin's motionless form.

'I...I'm sorry; we had no idea he was so—'

She cuts me off. 'What is it you want?'

'You don't need to be afraid of me.'

'Afraid of you? Why would I be afraid of you?'

'Well, rumour is that I killed your son-in-law.'

'Will you keep your voice down?' Edith shuts the door. 'I assumed you were here because you got your memory back.'

'Not all of it. I think I'm missing some important pieces.'

She studies me for a moment. 'Clearly.' Settling on the chair next to his bed, she clutches her husband's hand.

'I'm sorry,' Andrea says. 'The newspapers claimed he was on the mend. We never would have come if we'd known he was so ill.'

'They would say that because that's what we told them. I won't have the vultures circling his business. Not when there is still hope.'

My heart aches for her. The beeping machines and swooshing of his oxygen mask speak of anything but hope. 'I'm sorry. We'll get out of your way.'

Edith frowns at me. 'But you haven't asked your questions yet. Don't you want to know why you were created? Isn't that why you came here?'

'It's okay. I kind of assumed anyway.'

'You did?'

'Sure. You wanted to know what happened to Robert, and the facility offered you a way to do that. I might do the same if someone I loved disappeared.'

One side of Edith's mouth tugs up in a crooked smile. 'I hated that leech.'

'I thought you cared about Robert.'

'No, you didn't. Well, at least Nathan didn't. He knew my feelings towards Robert. It was Martin who thought the sun shone out of his backside. But even he saw him for what he was towards the end.'

'Did Martin tell you about his plan to have Nathan cloned?' Andrea asks.

'Not at first. I think he was worried I'd stand in his way. Martin would have done anything to give Julia closure. Fifteen years. That's how long she's been searching, wasting her life on that parasite who had every intention of casting her aside and moving on to his next victim. We had to know what happened to Robert for her sake.'

'But you already know,' Andrea says. 'Nathan was convicted.'

'Yes, he was. But sometimes the law gets it wrong.' She turns to me again. 'I don't feel good about how it ended for Nathan, you know.'

'What do you mean?'

'I prayed every night that Robert would just disappear. And he did. But so did a lot of money belonging to Martin's clients.'

'You thought Robert ran off with it?'

'I thought it was a possibility. But that little tart Leona claimed that wasn't the case. She said, although that had been his plan, Robert had got cold feet. Her crocodile tears were sickening. I didn't believe for a second that Robert was actually missing.'

'So how did Nathan factor into all of this?'

'He would neither confirm nor deny he had done the job. He told me to keep my money. But when the police tracked him down, he confessed. It made no sense.'

'The job?' Andrea gasps, and I will my brain to catch up with hers. 'You paid Nathan to kill Robert?'

'Wouldn't you? Coercive control, that's what they call it nowadays. I call it bullying. He made Julia's life hell. To protect her, I'd dispose of a thousand Roberts.'

My mind reels. So Nathan wasn't some crazy stalker. He was a hitman. 'Why are you admitting to all of this? We could tell the police.'

'Don't be foolish. You don't even exist. Do you know how easy it would be for me to dispose of you if you tried? And in answer to your question – guilt, I suppose. That's why I'm telling you. Not over Robert, but for what happened to Nathan.'

'Didn't he get what he deserved?' Andrea asks. 'After all, he was still a murderer. I doubt Robert was his only victim.'

It's as if her question has teeth, and it sinks them into my heart.

She must have sensed my pain because she adds, 'I'm sorry, Ryan, but it's true.'

'Maybe' Edith says. 'But I'm not whiter than white myself. Besides, like I said, I'm not certain he did kill Robert. Part of me still thinks my son-in-law is sunning himself on a private island somewhere.'

'Why would Nathan confess to something he didn't do?' I ask.

'I don't know. Either way, I should have done more to keep him alive. As soon as he was arrested, I washed my hands of him. Which, in a strange way, has worked in your favour.'

'Why?'

'You're my chance at redemption, Ryan. I let my husband pay for you to be created with one proviso. After we find out what happened to Robert, I get to decide what happens to you.'

I swallow a lump that has formed in my throat. 'And that is?'

'Fulfil your end of the bargain. Find out what happened to Robert. Do that and you'll be a free man. And a rich one at that.'

Chapter Twenty-One

The rumble of the engine does little to fill the silence between us. We both avoided pointing out the obvious on the way down in the elevator; whether Nathan killed Robert or not, he was not the innocent scapegoat we'd hoped.

'What now?' Andrea asks, and I grimace because I have no idea. 'Don't worry. Look, it's late. We'll go back to the apartment, get some rest and give it some thought.'

'I'm not a bad person, you know. No matter what Nathan did, how many people he killed, that isn't me. I won't turn into him.'

'I know.' She forces a smile, and it hurts more than if she told me outright that she didn't believe me.

'Well, you'll see soon enough anyway. How many days do I have left before I'm supposed to turn?'

'Tomorrow will be day five. Very few clones make it to day seven without...without reverting to type.'

'That's a very clinical way of putting it. You could also say without going bat shit crazy.'

'I could. But I didn't.'

I stare out the window as the sun drops below the Savannah skyline. Pinks and oranges melt together. It's beautiful, and I wonder if I will remember this if I become Nathan. It's hard to believe I will disappear completely. Maybe I will become the little voice at the back of his head, telling him no. The good angel on his shoulder.

Andrea pulls up. 'We got a space right outside the building. See, our luck is changing already.'

I follow her in and up the stairs. As she unlocks the door, she says, 'You investigate the food situation while I change.' She tosses her coat over the back of a chair.

My head is inside the empty fridge when I hear her phone ringing. 'Andrea!' She doesn't answer, so I fish inside her pocket for it. I pull it out along with a piece of paper. The screen of her cellphone displays the name *Andrew*. Andrew and Andrea. How quaint. I stab the reject call button and shove it back into her pocket.

The paper I hold is the same thick cream type as that inside my folder. I glance at the bedroom door but there is no sign of her. Unfolding the paper, I see my – Nathan's – name at the top. Below, in the same block font, is listed the details of his wife and child, Audrey and Gina. I know they aren't mine, but still a crushing sorrow weighs on me at the thought of having left them behind.

I flick open the folder at Nathan's parents' details. How did I miss the jump in the page numbers that followed?

'Because you weren't looking for it.' Nathan's mouth is so close to my ear that his breath sends a tingle down my neck.

I drop the folder and scramble away from him. 'You aren't real, are you?'

'No, not any more. They killed me. But let's get back to your original question. Why didn't you notice the missing page?' He pauses as if he's expecting me to answer.

'I don't know.'

'Of course you do.'

'Because...because Andrea gave me the file.'

'Exactly. Andrea gave you the file, and she's to be trusted. Isn't she?'

'Yes. She saved me.'

'Hmmm.' Nathan purses his lips in mock thought. 'Maybe she did. Maybe she didn't.'

'I was there. Have you considered that she didn't notice either?'

'The page was in her pocket, genius.'

My mouth feels dry. 'There could be a simple explanation.'

'Yes, like she doesn't trust you, that she thinks if you know about our family—'

'Your family.'

'Whatever. If we know about them, then they could be in danger.'

'No. She knows that I'm not like y—'

'Ryan.' Andrea is standing in the doorway to the bedroom, her eyes wide. 'Who are you talking to?'

I look around but Nathan is gone. 'Nobody. There's nobody here.'

'You saw Nathan, didn't you?'

I ignore her question and counter with one of my own.

'Why were you hiding this from me?' I wave the cream paper.

'Give me that.'

'I have a family.'

'No! Nathan had a family.'

I take a deep breath and try to steady my nerves. 'They could answer so many questions.'

'It's against protocol to involve the families. Besides, don't you think they've been through enough?'

I take a step back towards the door. 'But we aren't following facility protocol, are we? Because I'm free of the facility, right?'

Andrea's face drops. 'I just meant...It isn't fair to...'

I pull the gun from my waistband. 'Hand me your car keys.'

'Don't do this.' She tosses them to me, and then spreads her palms in front of her face as though she thinks she could catch a bullet. 'Ryan, please! I promise...'

I am already through the door and running before I can hear the end of the sentence.

Chapter Twenty-Two

Can I even drive this thing? I wonder as I turn the key in the ignition.

'Not legally,' Nathan answers me from the back seat. 'But you know how to point and go.'

I swivel round in my seat and grab for him. I find only empty air.

'Temper, temper.' He cackles. 'Why are you blaming me? The way I see it, I'm the only one who has actually been honest with you.'

I look at him in the rear view mirror, and he looks as real as anybody passing on the street around me. 'Because you're a stone cold killer, that's why.'

'I suppose I can't deny the killer part. But stone cold? No, I have a lot of heart.'

'Somehow I doubt your victims thought that.'

He shrugs. 'Probably not. Life is all about perspective though, isn't it?'

'Why can't I see you except in the mirror?'

'Don't ask me. This is all in your head.'

Relief sweeps over me. 'So you're not real?'

He gives that same throaty laugh. 'Out of the two of us, who is the more real? The version who touched lives, for better or worse. Had a family. Or the one born from a test tube less than a week ago.'

'I'm real.'

'Sure you are. For now.'

'What does that mean?'

'It means there is only space for one of us in that head.'

'You plan to kill me?'

'On the contrary, this doesn't have to be a hostile takeover. It would be easier for both of us if you just slip away.'

'Never. Why would I—' A screeching fills my skull and I clamp my hands to my ears. 'Make it stop.' Then come the voices: men's, women's, young, old, threatening, bargaining, begging.

I promise you will pay for this.

You don't have to do this. I have money.

Please. What about my children?

'Make it stop,' I plead.

'If you like. Just know that is what I come with. If you decide you want us to be roommates, you get my memories, too. Every person I killed will put down roots in your mind. Is that what you want?'

Tears sting my eyes. 'What if I don't want you as a roommate either?'

'The way I understand it from that red head, neither of us get a choice. I'm coming in, whether you like it or not. Give it some thought while we drive.'

'Where to?'

'I'd like a little family reunion.'

I unfold the piece of paper. 'What's the point? They won't be able to see you.'

'Maybe not, but you'll be able to talk to them for me. Now, let's get going.'

Chapter Twenty-Three

'Pull over here.' Nathan points towards a rundown apartment block.

'You lived here? I thought hitmen were supposed to be paid well.'

'They could write a book on all the things you don't know about me.' Nathan smirks. 'But not for long.'

I choose not to let him goad me. 'So, what now?'

'We...we wait.'

'For what? Shouldn't we at least go up?'

He's silent.

'Hang on a minute. I'm not the only one having trouble with my memory, am I? You can't remember which apartment you live in.'

'Shut up.'

'It looks like the great Nathan Ryan isn't as in control as he thinks.' It's my turn to cackle.

'I said shut up!' My head flies forward, and I headbutt

the steering wheel. The impact makes the horn honk, and a teenage girl turns round and gives me the finger.

'Wow! Did you see what I made you do? Woo hoo! Who's in the driving seat now?'

I try to piece together what just happened; somehow Nathan forced me to ram my own head into the wheel. 'How did you do that?'

He wiggles his fingers. 'It appears I am the puppet master. Let's see just what I can do.'

'Or, we could get on with the job at hand,' I say, trying to change the subject. 'That girl, who thinks I'm a pervert thanks to you, is going into your building. Shouldn't we follow her before the door shuts?'

'Good idea.'

I get out of the car, and Nathan is suddenly standing next to me. 'Why can I now see you without the mirror?'

'Your guess is as good as mine, amigo.' He walks on ahead, quickly catching up with the girl.

I follow. 'Excuse me, hold the door, please.'

She looks me up and down. 'And who the hell are you? I mean, other than some dirty old man looking for jail bait.'

'I'm younger than I look. Besides, I wasn't beeping at you. Sorry about that.'

'No? Well, it's hard to tell how old you are with all of this going on.' She circles a finger in the general vicinity of my bandages.

'Yeah, I was attacked.'

Her face falls. 'Oh. I'm sorry. Did they catch the guy?'

'They did. He won't hurt anyone else.'

'Good. So who is you're visiting?'

'Audrey. Audrey Ryan.'

The girl's face darkens. 'And what business do you have with her?'

'I knew her late husband.'

'Oh. Well, she's in apartment 302. I'm going that way.'

It's only as we get into the lift that it occurs to me how quiet Nathan has been. He stands staring at his shoes while the lift ascends.

'This is the floor,' the girl says, and we follow her out.

'Thank you. I can handle it from here.'

She thuds on the door. 'I'm sure you can.' The o is missing from 302 and somebody has drawn it in with a marker. 'Mom, open up!'

The door is flung open. 'Will you please, for once in your life, remember your key?' The woman looks at me. 'Who are you?'

'I, um...I used to...'

'He says he knew the sperm donor,' the girl says. 'In case you didn't guess already, Nathan Ryan was my father. I use that in the loosest sense of the word, of course. I was two when he earned himself the injection.'

I can see Nathan shuffling in the periphery of my vision and empathy bubbles inside me. This can't be easy for him to hear.

'He wasn't much of a father before that either,' her mother adds. She stoops a little, and I can tell she's trying to glimpse around my bandages. 'So you knew Nathan?'

'Not well.'

'No. I suspect he was as much use to you as he was to us. Gina, go in and stir the stew before it cements itself to the bottom of the pan.'

Gina grumbles but does as she's told. When she's out of

earshot her mother adds, 'Even with the dressings, I can see you got his eyes, his jaw.'

'What...?' My fingers go to my face. 'Oh you think he was my father, too.'

'I'm not blind. But I don't blame you. Who would want to admit to having that scum as their father? Not that you have anything to be ashamed of. His sins are not yours; remember that.'

'Thank you. It's Audrey, isn't it?'

'Yep. I always knew Nathan wasn't the faithful type. I'm surprised more of his children haven't turned up on my doorstep over the years. Well, you have my sympathies, but this isn't a support group. You'll have to deal with whatever issues he left you with yourself. We've got plenty of our own.'

'I didn't come to ask anything of you. Except maybe information. The truth is, I'm not all that sure Nathan was guilty of murdering Robert Lyle.'

'He was guilty all right. The police showed me pictures of the lock up he kept. It was like a shrine to Lyle's wife.'

'Julia.'

'Yeah. Photographs, news reports, even a tube of her lipstick. He was obsessed. It only makes sense he killed the husband to clear a path to her.'

'Someone told me he might have been a hitman.'

The woman sniggers. 'Maybe. But Nathan was the type to hurt people for the fun of it. He would just see it as a bonus if he got paid. Look, I've got to go. I hope you make peace with who he was.' The door is nearly shut, so that I can see only one deep brown eye when she says, 'Remember, you aren't him. Even if he was your father, you can break the cycle. That's what Gina is doing.' The door clicks shut.

Nathan emits a low pitch growl that turns into a howl. 'That's what she's been telling my kid about me? She's raising her to think I was a monster.'

'Well, weren't you?'

'No!' Nathan slams his fist into the wall.

'Ow!' It is only as pain shoots from my knuckles, up my wrist, that I realise that it's my own fists that have struck it. 'Don't do that.'

'Come on. I'm going to prove to the world that I'm innocent.'

Chapter Twenty-Four

Back in the car, Nathan is in the passenger seat.

'Not hiding in the mirror any more, I see.'

'Why bother? I don't need to be afraid of you.'

The throbbing in my knuckles agrees with him. 'I'm sorry if what Audrey said upset you, but I'd appreciate it if you expressed it in a less painful way.'

'Upset me? She's poisoned my kid's mind against me.'

'I think you did that yourself.'

'Don't comment on things you don't understand.'

'Oh, I understand all right.'

'No you don't. But I'm going to school you.'

I reach for something near the handbrake of the car. For what, I have no idea, because it's Nathan propelling me forward. My fingers push down the cigarette lighter. 'What are you doing?'

'Teaching you a lesson.'

The lighter pops out, signalling that it's hot, and I remove it. The end glows orange. 'Please don't do it.'

Nathan forces me to put the lighter to my skin, and I hear it fizz through my scream. Mercifully, he takes it away quickly. 'Got the message yet?'

'Yes, please stop.'

'You are me. A watered down, weak version, sure, but still me. Given that fact, I deserve a little loyalty.' He jams the lighter back in its hole, and I notice he has a sheen of sweat over his upper lip.

'That hurt you too, didn't it?' I ask.

'It doesn't matter. You'd be surprised what a high tolerance for pain I have, and I'll endure that a thousand times over if necessary. Now, you're going to drive.'

'Where to?'

'I'll direct you. That's all you need to know for now.'

I pull away from the kerb, my hand still smarting.

'Go straight.' Nathan scouts the streets around us. 'Next left. No, I mean right.'

'Do you even know where we're going?'

'Of course I do. My memory is a bit fuzzy, is all. That's no surprise with you taking up space in my head.'

'It's my head.'

'Not for long. Wait! It was that turning back there.'

'How was I supposed to know that?' I blink, and all of a sudden I am in the passenger seat and Nathan is behind the wheel. 'How did you...? Get out of my body!'

Nathan smirks at me. 'I think it's best if I do the driving.'

'Not a chance.' I close my eyes and will myself back into my body with all my might. Nothing happens.

Nathan laughs. 'Still not back in Kansas, Dorothy?'

I try again, but he still has control. 'Please. You had your chance at life.'

'Did I? Because to me it feels like I was cheated out of it.' Nathan accelerates through a red light. 'It's nothing personal, kid. But if I'm disappearing into oblivion again, it won't be without a fi—'

There is a screech of brakes as a huge lorry swerves to avoid us. I clutch my seat, too terrified to even scream. The body of the lorry wraps around us like a horseshoe.

Without warning, I am back in my body. My knuckles are white as I grip the wheel. 'You could have killed us.'

'You're safe, aren't you?'

'Yes, and back where I belong. I guess that lorry broke your concentration.'

'Don't you worry, it'll get easier with practice. Then you will be surplus to requirements. Now, could you reverse us out of here? Unless you'd like me to do it?'

I do as he says, unwilling to risk being hijacked again. 'Where now?'

'Turn round, then head straight.'

We drive in silence for ten minutes before I realise where he is taking us. 'This is the way to Julia's house.'

'And?'

'I won't let you hurt her.'

'Really? And how exactly do you plan to stop me?'

'I...'

'Relax. If she tells the truth, then she'll be fine.'

'And what is the truth?'

He gnaws at his lip so hard it bleeds. I feel the sting on my own mouth. 'I'm not sure. But I'll know it when I hear it.'

'If you can't remember, how do you know she has anything to tell?'

'My gut.'

'Well, as long as we're being logical. How did I come from you?'

'Believe me, I've been asking myself that same question.'

We pull up outside Julia's house. 'What now?' I ask.

'Knock on the door, I guess.'

I do as I'm told.

Julia appears. 'I've said everything I intend—'

Suddenly I am standing next to her. I watch, helpless, as Nathan barges into the house and clutches his hand over her mouth.

'Nathan, you maniac,' I yell. 'Leave her alone.'

The gun is pressed into the small of her back. 'Do you feel that?' he asks. 'I swear to God, if you make a fuss, I will shoot you. Understand?'

She nods.

'Good. Now I'm going to remove my hand, and you are going to behave. Got it?'

She nods again. A faint whimper escapes her as he pulls his hand away.

'Walk to the car.' Nathan stays close behind her, the gun still in place. 'Get in the passenger side.' He clambers into the driving seat.

I'm suddenly in the back seat of the car. I wonder if this is what it's been like for Nathan, suddenly transported close to wherever I was.

Julia swipes away a tear. 'Why are you doing this?'

'Because you're lying. It didn't happen how you said it did.'

Julia hesitates. 'Nathan? It is you. They told me it was a possibility that you would surface in the clone, but I never dared hope.'

Hope? That word echoes around my head.

She places her hand on his arm. 'You don't need a gun. Not with me. Where are we going?'

Nathan lowers the weapon but doesn't let go of it. 'To look at the ocean.'

Julia's eyes widen. 'We're reunited for the first time in years, and that's where you want to take me?'

'It seems fitting. That's where I last saw you. It might help me...clarify a few things.'

'There's no need. I can tell you whatever you want to know right now.'

He ignores her and starts the engine.

Chapter Twenty-Five

Nathan pulls up in a car park. 'Yes, this is it.'

'Why are we here?' Julia asks. 'There's no point raking up the past. We can be together now. It can be a fresh start.'

An image jumps into my head. Julia's hand is on my chest. No, Nathan's chest. She's looking up at him, smiling. Then they kiss. 'You two were involved?'

'Yes,' Nathan says. 'I remember now. She told me we could be together if I got rid of Robert.'

'She?' Julia looks around the car. 'Who are you talking to.'

Nathan sniggers. 'Myself. It's all coming back to me now, Julia. You knew he planned to leave you and run off with that woman. But the Hudsons don't lose, do they? You asked to speak to him, here, where he proposed.' Nathan opens the car door. 'Get out.'

Julia clambers from the car. 'Don't do anything stupid. We have another chance.'

I am standing right next to him. 'Whatever she did, don't sink to her level.'

'Sink to? Ryan, you're an idiot. I was born at that level. The only place I had to go was up. But that doesn't mean I'm going to let her get away with this.'

Julia's eyes dart around the car park, perhaps looking for help, but it's deserted.

'Don't get any ideas,' Nathan says. 'Walk.'

'Where to?' But there is something in the waver in her voice that tells me she knows.

'To the finale of course. Where it all ended the first time.' Nathan grabs her by her bicep and drags her forward.

'Nathan, please, you're hurting me.'

'Do you want to know what pain is? Pain is believing you wouldn't let me rot in prison. Pain is believing you'd step in before they killed me. What was it you said? 'My family are more powerful than Gods. Take the blame, and we'll have you out in no time."

As he speaks, pictures click over in my mind. The stalking part was true at least. But Julia was smart. She saw an opportunity when it presented itself. And Nathan really would have done anything for her.

'Here we are.' The three of us stand at the edge of a cliff. 'The scene of the crime. But not my crime. Isn't that right, Julia?'

I see it. It's so clear. She asked him to kill Robert, and at first he'd agreed. After all, her mother had already offered to pay him to do it. And it's not like it would have been the first man he'd killed. But something stopped him.

'I wanted to change.' Nathan says, and he's looking right at me.

'Are you seeing these images too?' I ask.

'Seeing them? I lived them. But yes, I remember it all now. When I told Julia that we should just let him go, she was furious. She had no intention of letting him get away with such disloyalty.'

'Look at it from my point of view.' Julia speaks through gritted teeth. 'I suffered years of abuse from him. The bullying, the gaslighting, and then, what, he was just going to cast me aside like a piece of rubbish? Never.'

'We'd have had each other.'

'No, I'd have been moving from one prison to another. You stalked me for months, Nathan. Is that really the basis for a healthy relationship?'

'So you were just using me?'

'I...I don't know. You have to understand, I was desperate. My whole life I've just been a possession, an accessory, to cruel and powerful men. My father, Robert...you.'

Nathan shoves her towards the cliff edge.

'No! Please!' Her feet are so close that rubble shifts and tumbles over the side. 'I just wanted to be free.'

'Don't do this,' I beg. 'Don't make me a murderer too.'

But he's not listening. 'Did you know I followed you here that day? Of course you did. I can't believe I was so naive.'

Julia's shoulders jerk as she heaves terrified breaths. 'Nathan, you're scaring me.'

'Am I? You weren't so scared last time I saw you here. Tell me, what did you say to get Robert up here?'

Julia sobs a garbled response.

Nathan inches her forward. 'Speak up. Young Ryan wants to hear too.'

She takes a few steadying breaths. 'I asked him to meet

me where he proposed, or I'd give my father all the evidence he needed to prove he'd embezzled his money.'

'A bluff, I'm sure. But that didn't matter. We both know Robert was never leaving this cliff.'

'It was an accident, I swear!'

Then I see it all. Julia and Robert are arguing. There are tears, from her at least. She grasps his shirt, and he looks down at her, tucks her hair behind her ear. He says something that I don't hear, because Nathan didn't hear it, and this is his memory. Robert tries to pull away but she won't let him. Julia stands on tiptoes and shouts something into his face. Then she shoves him. He staggers for a moment, flailing his arms at the cliff edge, before he plummets.

'What did you say to him?' Nathan asks. 'Right before you pushed him, I mean.'

'I said, 'If you want to go, then go'.' She's sobbing now. 'You don't know what it's been like for me this last fifteen years, living with the guilt over both of you, pretending to still search for him. If I could take it back, I would. I swear, I didn't plan to kill him.'

Nathan nods. 'At the time, I believed that. Not any more. How can I? You gave them my name. Did you care for me at —' Nathan jerks forwards, and for a sickening moment I think he is going to topple over. Instead, he staggers backwards, clutching his arm.

And then I am in my body again. There is blood on my palm. It oozes from the wound on my bicep. I have been shot.

Chapter Twenty-Six

I scan the cliff top and car park beyond. Half a dozen men, clothed from head to foot in black, appear from nowhere. Each has a rifle aimed at me.

'Shoot him!' Julia shouts. 'He was going to kill me.'

'No, I swear, that was Nathan. I'm Ryan.'

'They're not going to believe you.' Nathan stands behind Julia. 'That bullet jolted me out of you, but don't worry, I'll be back in control soon enough. Then you won't have to worry about any of this.'

'Julia.' I put my hands together, beseeching. 'You heard him talking to me. Tell them.'

'All I know is you're insane.'

'He's telling the truth.' Andrea pushes from between the line of men.

'Thank God.' I could cry with relief at the sight of her. 'How did you find me?'

'A tracker.'

'In the car?'

She presses her lips together so tightly that they seem to disappear, the truth trapped behind them.

'It's in me, isn't it? They've known where I am this entire time.'

'Yes,' she says. 'We needed Nathan to lead us here. It was the only way he'd give away the location of the body.'

I look at Julia. Her eyes are puffy from crying.

'Yes,' I say. 'This is where he did it.'

Nathan roars. 'You lying scum. Tell them it was her!'

'No,' I say. 'You owe her this.'

'Ryan, are you speaking to Nathan now? Is he still here?'

'Yes.'

'You can both take control over the same body. Fascinating.'

'That's not the word I'd use for it.' It's only now that I notice the change in Andrea. Her hair is twisted into a neat bun. Her crumpled scrubs have been traded for a sharp suit. 'What's happened to you?'

'Nothing. You don't need to worry, Ryan. I'm here to help.'

'Aren't you in trouble for letting me escape?'

Nathan chuckles. 'You're so damn dumb. They wanted you to escape.'

'You can't know that. How can you?'

'Because I see what's in front of me. You only see what you want to see. She's been playing us since the beginning.'

'No. That isn't true.'

Andrea takes a step towards me. 'Ryan, what is Nathan saying?'

'He's saying I can't trust you.'

'I'm your friend. Of course you can.'

'Then why did you let them shoot me?'

'To save Julia. But only in the arm. We'll soon patch you up.'

'Why?'

'What do you mean?'

'Why patch me up when they're just going to kill me anyway?' I see now; there is no way out of this for me. Edith Hudson's promise was likely a lie, and even if it wasn't, Julia would never let her fulfil it. Not if it meant Nathan would be free to terrorise her.

Andrea sighs. 'Nobody is going to kill you. I won't let them.'

'Like you have any say over that.'

Andrea smiles. 'I have *all* the say over that, Ryan. I'm not just a technician. Actually, I'm in charge of this whole operation. I'm sorry I had to mislead you—'

'Lie to me.'

'But I needed you to trust me. You have no idea how important you are.'

'So you could find Robert's body.'

'At first, yes. But you are the first specimen that has fought their original.'

'I'm not a specimen. I'm a person.'

'Yes, that's exactly my point. We thought the clones were just empty vessels waiting to be filled. But you, you were your own person from the start. Come back with me, let us study you, and we'll find a way to exorcise Nathan for good.'

I long to believe her, but I'm not convinced. It's impossible to ignore the way Nathan's memories surfaced within me.

'You're right,' Nathan says, reading my mind. 'It's only a

matter of time. Do you think I was born a monster? Whether they get rid of me or not, you'll follow my path.'

'I can't let that happen.' I take a step towards the edge of cliff.

'Let what happen?' Andrea asks. 'Just come with me. Let me help you.'

'I'm the only person that can help me.' I look over at the crashing waves as they batter the rocks below.

'Don't even think about it,' Nathan says. 'I was wrong. We can find a way to live together.'

I take my last look at him, the man I'm destined to become. 'Don't tell me what to do.' Then I jump for the final time.

The Book of Jared
Chapter 1

Read on for chapter 1 of 'The Book of Jared', the first in the Escaping Sanctuary series.
<u>Escaping Sanctuary:</u>
<u>The Book of Jared</u>

This is the end. I do not blame you if you feel cheated. Nobody expects to open a book at the first page and discover that the story has happened without them.

I could have begun my tale with superstorms and flash floods. Perhaps you'd have enjoyed hearing of hail so big that it crushed cars or tornadoes that demolished cities.

But then I'd be cheating you in a different way. I was a small child when all of that happened. Climate change was whispered about over my head at the dinner table and reported on news bulletins that I wasn't allowed to watch. But there was only so long that they could shield me from such worries before they became my own. Though, I don't want to talk about that.

The day we were led below ground was the closing act. I stole a final glimpse of the rectangle of light as the door closed behind us. I would have looked for longer had I realised it would be the last hint of daylight I would see for years.

But every ending allows a new beginning, and that is where my story starts.

Edmond

The alarm blared, sending Edmond rushing from his unit. 'What's happening? David?'

'Give me a minute.' David spoke in frantic whispers to the security team, sending them racing towards the entryway. 'Walk!' David yelled after them. 'And will someone please shut off that alarm! We don't want the citizens panicked before they even get down here.'

'David, what's going on?'

'It's nothing to worry about.'

'Don't do that. I'm not some doddery old man that needs your protection. Tell me.'

'Fine. We've had reports of intruders at the perimeter fence.'

'Is it them?' Edmond didn't want to dirty himself by saying the word. Cannibals. But that's exactly what they were. They'd already lost one team to them. Edmond had visited the scene and witnessed the devastation left behind. He'd owed that much to their families. After all, he'd sent them on that mission. But those images would be scorched into his memory forever. Bones stripped clean, discarded innards, he saw them whenever he closed his eyes.

'I don't know,' David said. 'But we proceed as planned. The guardians are going to patrol the boundary fence. There's no reason for the new arrivals to know anything about them.'

'Yes. You're right. There would be no point in scaring the citizens. It's just...'

'Edmond, what is it?'

'My family arrive today. My daughter, Laura and grandson, Jared. They are probably up there right now.'

'Oh. You didn't say anything.'

'I already bent the rules by adding them to the list. I thought it best to let them go through the usual entry—'

'Edmond.' David cut him off. 'This place only exists because of you. Why shouldn't your family get a little preferential treatment.'

'I suppose.'

'No question about it.'

'You're right.' Waves of anxiety washed over him. 'I should have been up there looking after them from the moment they stepped off the bus.'

David clutched his shoulders. 'Listen to me. Earthquakes, floods, sandstorms, your family will have faced plenty of dangers without you.'

Edmond bristled. 'Is that supposed to make me feel better?'

'I'm sorry. That came out wrong. I just mean, they must be tough to have got this far. They'll be able to wait a few hours without you babysitting them.'

'But the intruders—'

'Are likely nothing but some survivors looking to see what all the commotion around here is. The sooner we get everyone below ground and those doors locked, the better.'

'You're right.'

'I usually am. Let the guardians handle everything up there. You just focus on your speech. I'll make sure your family's group is processed next.'

'Thank you.'

'And Edmond? Stick to the script. Please. The citizens need to know the rules as soon as they arrive.'

'I'll do my best.'

David grumbled. 'I guess that will have to do.'

Laura

'I'll never forgive you.' Those were some of Laura's last words to her father, and she'd said them at her mother's wake.

If she was honest, she'd enjoyed how he'd flinched as they struck. *Good,* she'd thought. *You can experience just a little of my pain.*

'There was no way for me to know. If I had any inkling—'

'What? You would have cancelled your trip, and I wouldn't have missed out on seeing my mother for the last time? Unlikely. You've never put me first.'

'That's not true.' Edmond's eyes glistened, but not a single stubborn tear fell.

Laura doubled down on her efforts. 'Or maybe it wouldn't have happened at all.'

'Don't.' It was a warning, but if anything, it just drove Laura on.

'After all, she'd have been safe at home if it wasn't for your precious work.' She could tell by the way his face crumpled that it wasn't the first time that idea had occurred to him. 'It's true. If you hadn't asked her to go with you—'

'That's a wicked thing to say.' Edmond picked up a plate of sandwiches. 'We have guests waiting. When you want to discuss this like an adult, you know where I am.'

'Hell will freeze over first!' That's what she'd shouted after him before letting herself out the back door.

Laura knew how cruel she'd been. Many nights she'd lain awake, wishing she could take those words back.

Now, she just felt foolish. Because it turned out that hell

didn't need to freeze over for her to speak to him again. All it took was a run-of-the-mill earthquake, barely a level four on the Richter scale. Nothing compared to what they'd experienced over the last few years. But Laura never imagined that as the ground stopped shaking that day, the earthquake would take her partner with it.

Laura pushed the memories down. She couldn't dwell, not when she had a child to protect. And if that meant swallowing her pride and accepting her father's help, so be it. But she supposed, considering that last conversation, she could understand why he hadn't come to meet them when they'd first arrived at the camp outside the Sanctuary. Still, it stung.

It was past midday, and still they squatted under one of the makeshift tents, waiting to be called. Thirty-seven, that was the number her group had been assigned on arrival. With painful slowness, they'd announced the numbers over the speakers. The last she'd heard had been number eleven.

'How much longer do we have to wait?' Jared had been asking the same question on repeat since they'd arrived early that morning.

It had gone past grating and Laura was gnawing on the inside of her cheek to stop from snapping. 'As long as it takes. There are lots of people that arrived ahead of us.'

'But they've been calling our number for ages.'

'What? No, that can't be right.'

Laura poked her head from below the tarp to listen.

Group number thirty-seven, make your way to the entrance.

'You're right.' Laura scrabbled around on the floor, scooping their things into her backpack. 'What happened to numbers twelve to thirty-six.'

'That's what we were wondering.' The woman next to her glared, her three children perfectly mirroring her expression. Laura could understand. They'd already been waiting hours when she'd arrived.

'It's probably a mistake. You watch, I'll be back in a minute.' She prayed she was wrong.

They joined a line of people. Although she recognised many of the faces from the coach, she'd exchanged little more than mumbled pleasantries with any of them. Now she beamed at them as the queue moved steadily forward.

'Is that the Sanctuary?' Jared asked. 'It's not very big.'

'Most of it is underground, remember.'

They'd camouflaged the entrance within a looming wall of black. Laura supposed it was a fitting choice for a mine. Still, she wished for some buttercup yellow or flamingo pink, already mourning the palette she would leave behind. It was a shame to be led through black into more black.

In contrast, the guards who stood securing the entrance wore a vibrant blue. They nodded as Laura's group passed.

A guide met them just outside the main door. 'I'm Jennifer, and it is my privilege to welcome you to the Sanctuary. I must warn you that the stairs are an original feature of Wieliczka Salt Mine. They have been checked and reinforced by the best engineers in the world. But still, I admit that three hundred and fifty wooden steps left me a bit wobbly when I first saw them.'

Laura glanced down at Jared, ready to reassure him, but she needn't have worried. He was standing on tiptoes, impatient to see what was inside. 'Come on, Mum.' She wondered if he'd be so enthusiastic if he realised all that he was leaving behind.

'Give me just a second.' Laura took a last look up at the sun. Born into the endless British drizzle, once it would have taken the slightest nudge of the thermometer for her to join the wave of people heading for the beach, shedding layers of clothing as they went.

But then, of course, the Levelling ended all of that. Humans no longer ruled; they survived. The sun had become a cruel master. Merciless, it hung above them, a constant threat.

For the longest time, Laura tried to secure herself and Jared in a bubble of denial. Switching the channel and leaving the newspapers unread let her believe, just for a little while, that they weren't quite as vulnerable as she feared.

Jared followed her gaze. 'Nicholas Copernicus – 1543. He was the first to say that the planets orbited the Sun. Did you know that?'

'I did not.' She pushed red waves of unruly hair from his eyes. 'Are you ready?'

'Yes.' He shook the hair back into his face.

'Then let's take a look at our new home.' Laura took a deep breath as they were led through the heavy metal door, into the unknown.

Jennifer hadn't been exaggerating. The steps coiled and twisted below, making Laura's stomach lurch. She clutched the wooden bannister.

'That's a long way down.' Jared sounded impressed rather than scared.

They began their descent, manoeuvering their bulky backpacks into the narrow stairwell.

'The original mine reached a depth of three hundred and twenty-seven metres.' Jennifer spoke into the gloom, her words barely reaching Laura, let alone the twenty or so people who trailed behind them. 'Looking at the entrance, you would have little idea just how far it spreads below Krakow. The original salt mine covered over two hundred and eighty-seven kilometres. However, during the construction of the Sanctuary, that number was more than doubled.'

At the bottom of the stairs, they entered a cavernous chamber of unpolished salt rock. Laura was surprised to realise it wasn't the crystal white she once scattered over her meals.

Wooden barriers lined the side of the chamber. Jared raced to look over. 'Isaac Newton – 1664.'

A huge drop still loomed below them. Nausea twisted Laura's guts, but she forced a cheery tone. 'Even I know that one, smarty pants. But I'm trying my best not to think about gravity, right now.'

'How far do you think it goes down?' Jared picked up a salt rock chip and dropped it over.

'I have no idea.'

'A good question, young man.' Jennifer stamped her foot. 'There is still a drop of over two hundred metres below us. If I were to take you to the lowest part of the mine, you would have to descend eight hundred steps spread across nine levels.' Laura's pallid complexion must have been clear despite the poor light because Jennifer added, 'Don't worry. You are perfectly safe. What you can't see are the tonnes of iron and steel supporting the structure from beneath.'

Jennifer directed them through one of the arches flanking the cavern and they found themselves in a tunnel. Laura let her fingers trail along the cool salt rock. Goosebumps rose on her skin, an enjoyable sensation after the endless heat.

The woman in front of them squealed and sprung back, landing heavily on Laura's foot. She didn't bother to apologise as she stepped forward again. Then she let out a chuckle. 'It's not real.'

Jared moved closer to her. 'What is it?'

Laura squinted to make out the two mannequins, positioned in a recess carved out of the rock. They wore white overalls, suspended for ever with their shovels scraping away at the ground. *Tough gig*, Laura thought. *Not even a coffee break.*

But to Jared, she said, 'Just a left-over exhibit, I think. In his letter, your grandfather said this place was used as a tourist attraction after the mine closed. I guess they were feeling sentimental when deciding what to keep.'

They continued down the passageway, peering at the tableaux staged in the recesses of the walls. The first figure stoked a fire, poking at faux embers that were backlit by an eerie artificial light. The next led a horse and cart, its hooves forever frozen mid-trot, a snapshot of a world alien to her.

At the end of the tunnel, Jennifer stopped. 'I'm afraid we have some final checks to do before you become official citizens of the Sanctuary. Nothing for you to worry about. It's all very routine.' Laura wondered if Jennifer was trying to persuade them or herself. By the furtive glances other members of the group exchanged, she could see they were wondering the same thing.

As they left the tunnel, the space widened, and they found a row of three desks. A clerk sat behind each one, checking the details of the new arrivals. Each citizen was processed and waved through with well-oiled efficiency.

Laura and Jared took their place in one of the queues. The woman behind the desk wore a silver name badge etched with the name 'Stacey'.

Laura heard raised voices from the queue to her right.

'But we've come all this way.' As the woman's volume increased, the pigtailed toddler clutching her leg buried her face in the material of her skirt.

'Just stand to one side, and somebody will come and speak to you.'

'No. No, I won't.' She squared her shoulders.

The clerk beckoned to the uniformed officers standing to the side.

One of them took the woman by the arm. 'Come with me, please.'

She paled. 'Just let us get settled in and I will come back and answer any questions you have. Or at least send Bella through.' She smoothed a hand over the back of the child's blonde head.

'We can't admit an unaccompanied child into the Sanctuary. Come with me, and we will get this sorted.' The officer guided her away from the line. The woman scanned the queues as she left, perhaps hoping for help.

Laura was embarrassed to be caught staring and looked away. Turning back to the desk, she realised Stacey was talking to her.

'Names, please?' The irritation in Stacey's voice suggested it wasn't the first time she'd asked.

'Oh. Sorry. Laura Pearse and Jared Morgan.'

Stacey tapped the names into a tablet. She scrolled through multiple pages and her brow knitted.

The people in the next queue were approved and allowed to enter. Then the group after them.

Laura gnawed at the inside of her mouth. 'Is everything okay?'

'Absolutely.' Stacey's smile was too bright, unconvincing. 'I just need to check something.' She waved over a man, and they exchanged whispers, throwing furtive glances back over at Laura.

'Is there a problem?'

'Laura Pearse,' the man read from the screen. 'And Jared Morgan. You have different surnames.'

Laura resisted the urge for sarcasm. 'Yes. His father and I weren't married. Is that a problem?'

'Well...' His incomplete sentence confirmed that it was. He flicked through further screens, before pausing. 'Your father is Edmond Pearse.'

'Does that make any difference?'

He handed the tablet back to his colleague. 'Welcome to the Sanctuary.'

Laura's heart picked up its regular rhythm. It hadn't occurred to her that they could still be turned away, let alone for something so irrelevant.

'One last task.' Stacey brought a stamp down, hard, on Laura's hand.

Needles punctured her skin. 'What was that?' Laura ran her thumb over the small lump it left behind.

'Your tracker. Everybody in the Sanctuary is required to have one.'

Laura looked closer at the stinging patch on the back of

her hand. A small 'S' lay in the middle of the aggravated skin. 'You can't just do that without asking.'

Stacey's smile didn't falter. 'I can if you want entry to the Sanctuary. You do, don't you?'

Laura looked at Jared. His fist was clutched around his father's lucky coin. He always carried it with him, holding it like a comfort blanket.

'Yes,' Laura whispered.

'Good. The boy next.'

'What? I'm not going to let you brand my child.'

'It only stings for a second. As you know.' Stacey looked at Jared. 'Besides, these chips are magic, so you'll definitely want one. It has a translator inside. You'll be able to talk to all the new friends you make, whether you speak the same language or not. Isn't that amazing?'

Laura knew Jared was listening, that later he would explain in minute detail his theories on how he thought the chip must work. But to Stacey, as Jared scuffed the toes of his shoes against the floor, it must have looked like he was ignoring her. Laura wished she had that option. Instead, she leaned forward and whispered to Jared: 'It's okay. I hardly felt it.'

Jared eyed her with suspicion. Laura didn't blame him. She had little experience with comforting him; that had always been Mark's area. Since his death, she'd stumbled from one clumsy parenting move to another.

To her surprise, Jared offered Stacey his hand. When she finished, he rubbed at the same blue tattoo. 'What does the 'S' mean?'

'STEM,' Stacey said, stamping each document on the

tablet with her thumbprint before flicking it aside. 'It's short for science, technology, engineering and mathematics.'

'Oh, there must be a mistake,' Laura said. 'I'm not a scientist or anything. I was a medical rep. I worked in sales.'

'I know.' Stacey raised one eyebrow. 'But your father is.'

Laura's face flushed at the implied nepotism.

'If you don't mind.' Stacey looked pointedly at the queue of people behind her.

Laura pulled on her backpack, but before she left the desk, she noticed a red 'T' on Stacey's hand. 'What does that stand for?'

'Trade,' she said, with a huff. 'Anybody who isn't in STEM research or a benefactor to the Sanctuary is lumped under the term 'trade'.' She screwed her lips into a pout.

'Sorry. I'll get out of your way.' Laura wasn't sure whether she was apologising for the delay or the unearned 'S' on her hand.

The Book of Jared

'Let's take a look at our new home.' That's what my mother said as we stepped into the gloom of the stairwell.

Our home. Those two words circled my brain.

Back on the surface, home had been so much more than four walls and a roof. It was built from the scraps of our history. It was stitched together with shared experiences and endured sorrows.

Home was not the three bedrooms and two bathrooms that we left behind. It was the footprints tattooed onto our front path. My six-year-old brain hadn't been able to resist the temptation of the wet concrete. To this day, I can feel the suction as it caked the soles of my shoes. I can still hear the squelch as I pulled my feet free, turning to stare at the footprints I'd left behind, panic rising as I realised they were not going to disappear.

When my father found me, hiding by the side of the house, he hadn't been mad. Instead, he planted his own shoes in the mixture right next to the outline of mine. 'Some things can't be undone,' he said. 'You're going to make mistakes. But when you do, know that you never have to hide them from me.' He pointed down at our footprints. 'No matter what, we're forever.'

So no, home wasn't the missing roof tiles or the peeling paint on the shed. It was the markings on the door frame that my mother had made on every one of my birthdays, my father and grandmother clapping me on as if I had any control over the outcome.

The home we once had wasn't defined by our untidy lawn, alive with dandelions and not much else. It was the cracked windowpane, which my parents had often talked of having repaired, that made it ours. I don't think they really wanted to change it at all. Discussing it was just an excuse to bring up my grandmother's attempt to teach me how to play ball. It was her that broke the window, by the way.

After I lost my father and grandmother, all that had made that house a home disappeared. The warmth and light that I remember filling those airy rooms abandoned us.

You could say that by the time we reached the Sanctuary, I'd been homeless for a long time. So it seemed as good a place as any to start again.

For more information on 'The Book of Jared',
click on the link below or scan the QR code.
<u>Escaping Sanctuary:</u>
<u>The Book of Jared</u>

www.ingramcontent.com/pod-product-compliance
Lightning Source LLC
Chambersburg PA
CBHW030804190726
48285CB00003B/1018